# Next, on a very special *That Ghoul Ava…*

(The REAL 3rd book of the *That Ghoul Ava* series…unless you count those two short stories.)

## TW Brown

https://www.facebook.com/pages/Author-TW-Brown

Portland, Oregon, USA

**Next, on a very special *That Ghoul Ava...***
©*2014 May December Publications LLC*

Printed in the U.S.A.

ISBN -9781940734279
LCCN

Printed in the United States of America.

# More Titles From May December Publications

### The Ava Series by TW Brown

That Ghoul Ava: Her First Adventures
That Ghoul Ava and The Queen of the Zombies
That Ghoul Ava Kicks Some Faerie A**

### The Dead Series by TW Brown

Dead:The Ugly Beginning book 1
Dead: Revelations book 2
Dead: Fortunes and Failures book 3
Dead: Winter book 4
Dead: Siege and Survival book 5
Dead: Confrontation book 6
Dead: Reborn book 7
Dead: Darkness Before Dawn book 8
Dead: Spring book 9
Dead: Reclamation book 10

### The Monster Squad Series by Heath Stallcup

Return of the Phoenix book 1
Full Moon Rising book 2
Coalation of the Damned book 3
Blood Apocalypse book 4

### The Zomblog Series by TW Brown

Zomblog book 1
Zomblog II book 2
Zomblog The Final Entry book 3
Zomblog: Snoe book 4
Zomblog: Snoe's War book 5
Zomblog: Snoe's Journey book 6

### Special Editions by TW Brown

DEAD: The Geeks
DEAD: Vignettes
DEAD:Steve's Story (Perspectives)
DEAD: Special Edition Compendium 1
DEAD: The Geeks 2

DEAD: Vignettes 2
DEAD:Perspectives 2
DEAD: Special Edition Compendium 2

Zomblog: Compendium 1
Zomblog Saga Box Set – complete set of Zomblog 1-6

### Stand Alone Titles

Dakota  by Todd Brown
Gruesomely Grimm Zombie Tales -1 by TW Brown
The Exoterrestrials by TW Brown

### Anthologies

A Clockworks Orchard: Rivets & Rain
Chivalry is Dead – all male authors
Dear Santa
Eye Witness: Zombie
First Time Dead
First Time Dead 2
First Time Dead 3
Four in the Hole
Fresh Blood
Hell Hath No Fury…all female authors
Midnight Movie: Creature Features
Midnight Movie: Creature Feature 2
Realms of the Undead
Say goodnight to the Bad Guy
Spiders
Vampires Aren't Pretty
Wake the Witch - our charity anthology – 100% goes to Red Cross
Zero
Zombie: Lockdown


# You can find our titles on Audio as well.

# Find them at Audible.com

*For the REAL Muffy!*

# A moment with the author…

Ava is my guilty pleasure. She started out as just a little something that I did as a "thank you" for one of my first ever fans. The thing is, I found that she had more going on than what I could put together in a short story. Ava was "alive"…or at least as alive as a ghoul can be.

Many of you know me for my *DEAD* and/or *Zomblog* series of books. This is about as far from these as you can get, and I appreciate how many of you have made the leap and discovered that you enjoyed my quirky ghoul-friend.

I make no bones about it…this is my entry into absolute commercial mainstream. As much as I would love to see some of my zombie stuff on the big or small screen, the fact is that they are probably not suited for that sort of thing. Ava is different.

However, believe it or not, there is a formula for success in this genre. I am blessed to have some wonderful women who provide me with ample feedback for this series. Among them is the lovely and talented Shana Festa, whose guidance in this project has been invaluable. She listened to my goals for Ava and helped create a game plan. (If success eludes me, the fault is solely mine…you have been a gem, Shay.)

In addition, I have to step aside and let the amazing Pamela Lorrence take a bow. She is the voice on the audio editions of the *That Ghoul Ava* series, starting with *That Ghoul Ava and The Queen of the Zombies*. She took this baby and made it hers and I could not be any happier.

There are my usual cast of characters to thank, but I would be remiss if I did not make mention that this book was completed during a family tragedy. My wife Denise lost her eighteen-year-old son to complications from diabetes just as this book was being wrapped up. The dedication was already set, but I want to also add that this book will be dedicated in the memory of John Douglas Skagen. I hope they have macaroni and cheese in Heaven, young man. His loss is a reminder of how short our time can be, and how you should live each day to the fullest and never let the sun set on your anger between you and those you love. Fortunately, Denise can have peace that her last communication with her son was a text that read, "Love you buddy."

There are always people to thank and I never get them all, so let me just toss out a list of a few people that make my life worth living: Ronni, Cody, Alex, Jenifer, Cindy, Jason, Doug and Jamie Smith, Erik and Kelly Rise, Edith (Mom) McKinzie, Beth "Muffy Bunny" Maffitt, Mike Ridenour. Vix and Ivor Kirkpatrick, Mark and Tracy, Armand, and most of all, my wife Denise who makes every day special.

*Gee, Brain, what do you want to do today?*
TW Brown
July 2014

# Contents

# 1

# Mystify

Happy endings are overrated. I'm just sayin'.

After a meeting with my ghost writer, Chantal, I have decided, against my better instincts, to agree and share this story. Chantal says that sometimes a dark chapter is important; it lets the readers know that the hero is not perfect. My immediate question to her in response was to ask if she'd been paying attention to my story so far. I mean, I have two actual books under my belt (not counting the pair of short stories that I put together when I was first embarking on this adventure). So far, I would not say that I have come out looking anything like a hero.

Remember the "Must See TV" craze that NBC had going on back in the day? It started in the 80s and carried over to the early 90s. One of the things that became a bit of a staple for the sitcom was the "Next time, on a very special [insert random sitcom title here]…" As soon as you heard that brooding voice over, you knew something bad was going to happen. Whether it was the perv who touched Arnold in his "bad place" on *Different Strokes*, or Tootie, Jo, Blair, and Natalie attending their first orgy, this was going to be one of those episodes that was light on laughs and heavy on the moral-of-the-story type stuff. (And I may have made up that last *Facts of Life* show idea, although I know a lot of teen boys who would have totally tuned in.)

This is what you might consider to be one of *those* stories. While I am sure that you will find more than a a fair share of moments that induce a roll of the eyes and make you think; *Oh, Ava, will you never learn?* This is one of those escapades that is short on the 'lighter side' and consists of more of the stuff that makes up real life. You know what I'm talking about; disappointment, screw ups, and compounding bad decision on bad decision.

What? I'm the only one who does that? Hmm. Oh well, then I guess this will simply give you another reason to feel better about yourself at my expense.

During my little break after all of the excitement with the faeries, I did something I am not exactly proud of: I read. Now before all you literacy types get your panties bunched up, (not to mention the irony of me admitting that I hate reading as you sit comfortably someplace reading *this* book), I am just admitting a fact. Yes, I am a visual medium kind of girl...sue me! Although I have taken to listening to audio books lately, so a big thanks to whatever genius came up with that idea. Oh, am I blathering on? Sorry. Back to my reading.

That being said, I read a bunch of my contemporaries. I read Sookie, Anita, and Amanda. All I can say is that I must be doing it all wrong. These gals have men—or vampires, werewolves and the like—pawing at them all the time. And judging by the descriptions...it is always hunky types with six pack abs. What do I get?

Sure, I had a vampire beau for a while, but vamps smell like hot garbage to a ghoul, so that was not all it was cracked up to be. No matter, since he is nothing but dust now. Oh...and I have an obscenely disproportionately endowed goblin named Nose Wart who sticks to me like glue.

That was why I was so surprised when I was sitting on a bench at Washington Park just trying to enjoy the first blooms of all the rose bushes. They call Portland the Rose City for a reason. For those of you not in the know, roses are to Portland what peaches are to Georgia, beans to Boston, and cowboy hats to Texas. I had no idea how drastically my life was about to change.

So, the next time you reach one of those forks, don't rush to make a choice. You don't get to go back and redo your decision. I really wish those sorts of things had big flashing signs that let you know how important they are in shaping your future.

Anyway, there I was just sitting on the bench...

\*\*\*

"Are you Ava Birch?"

I looked up to see a really tall man standing there.

My surprise came from a few places. For one, with my senses being what they are, nobody sneaks up on me. And even if this guy was a Supernatural, his height should have made him jump out of the background which consisted mostly of skater types playing Hackey Sack or mushy couples walking hand in hand with stupid expressions of love plastered on their faces as they enjoyed the pleasantly warm spring night. (Am I a bit of a pessimist when it comes to romance? You bet.)

"Who's asking?" I shot back.

For added effect, I let my sunglasses slip down to reveal my all black orbs. When the guy did not so much as flinch, I was pretty sure he was part of the "community." Now I would have to find out just what sort of creature he was.

"My name is not of any importance, I come with the mind to divert or stop a matter of grave danger to all of us," he said as he took a seat on the bench beside me.

"Seriously, can't you people just spit out whatever it is you want? You all sound like bad Shakespearean actors at summer stock."

As I spoke, I was using every sense that I had. The problem was that I kept coming up empty. He had no noticeable smell. That was a surefire indication that he wasn't human. Every human has a smell. You are all slowly dying, some perhaps not slow enough and others much faster than you might realize. The closer you are to death, the stronger your scent. And since I eat the dead, you basically become more and more yummy to me as

3

you approach the end of your mortal life.

Very few things offer up nothing in the way of smell. So far, Morgan and Blue being the most notable. Psychics are still a mystery to me. They have no smell and can creep up on me without giving themselves away.

"Are you a psychic?" I blurted. It wasn't loud, just sudden. Still, the man acted like I had just pressed a button that lit a neon sign with giant arrows that pointed directly at him.

"Perhaps we can go someplace a bit more private." The stranger's voice was an odd rasp that came in a whisper that I was certain nobody would be able to overhear unless they were a Supernatural.

"Sure." I shrugged and got up.

Inside, I had to chuckle at the idea of simply agreeing to go "someplace a bit more private" with this absolute stranger. That usually ended poorly for any woman who acted with such foolish disregard. Honestly, I am surprised that the news is not full of more horror stories with all the online dating services becoming so common. However, anybody who might have bad intentions towards me would find themselves biting off more than they could chew.

Actually…if I thought about it, I would be the one doing the biting. The more I thought about it, the harder it was to contain. I really tried, but I could not keep it in. A snorting chuckle escaped my lipes that sounded a lot like Chrissy Snow from *Three's Company*.

"What do you find humorous?" The man placed a much-too-familiar hand on my elbow as we wove through the Royal Rose Garden and made our way to the Hoyt Arboretum. To his credit, he let go once I glared hard enough.

"Do you make it a habit of approaching strange women and asking them to wander off into the woods?" I said with as much seriousness as I could muster…which, admittedly, was not very much.

The man stopped so suddenly that I literally ran into his back. I felt something under his coat that felt like knobs; sort of like those bumpers you find on a bumper pool table…or maybe mushrooms made out of granite. When he spun to face me, I noticed that his eyes had taken on a silvery color.

"That's a neat trick." I took an instinctive step back and willed my trusty switchblade fingers to pop out.

"What?" He seemed puzzled and then blinked a few times, clearing his eyes back to what were now just puppy dog brown. "I apologize…let me begin again."

"Seriously, dude, you haven't really begun in the first place."

"My name is Mystify."

The man stuck out a hand. I noticed right away that he had some unnaturally long fingers that I bet were a real bitch when it came to finding gloves that would fit properly. Seriously, they were freakishly long digits. I guess my focus on his fingers is why it took me a few seconds to catch what he had given as his name.

"Excuse me?" Maybe I'd heard him wrong.

"I said that my name is Mystify."

"Uh-huh."

"And your guess is correct, I am indeed a psychic. To be more specific, I am on the council that oversees all of the psychics throughout the world."

"So you are like Morgan's boss." I said this as a statement more than actually asking it as a question. Perhaps I should not be so quick to make assumptions.

"Heaven's no," he said with a laugh that would chill the blood of a serial killer. "We do not operate quite like that. Our job is completely hands off…unless somebody has need of being replaced."

"Replaced? You mean like as in fired?" Yep, now I was asking what I felt were appropriate and pertinent questions. While I did not have warm and fuzzy feelings for Morgan the Psychic who was in charge of my region, it was a case of what my uncle always said about the devil you know versus the one that you don't.

"I had to see you for myself." Mystify ignored my question and was regarding me as if I might be some mishap in a research facility. "Many had thought that perhaps the ghouls would never return. So many of the bloodlines have been fouled over the millennia..."

"Bloodline? Wait, are you saying that this is genetic?" I might not be the sharpest knife in the drawer, but I'm not a total idiot.

"Not in the way you are thinking," Mystify said with a shake of his head. "It is more like a parasite that travels from host to host until it finds a suitable place to call home."

"Huh?" Yep, back to being a butter knife.

"Sorry." Mystify shook his head and returned his gaze to me.

He blinked, and the silver coating on his eyes was there again for a split second. So maybe it was like a second eyelid; that was the only deduction that I could come up with. But then, why hadn't I seen anything like that with Morgan? And what was hiding under the long duster he was wearing; I'd felt something very...knobby.

"I tend to think out loud, most of it is of no consequence."

I noticed how he said the word "most" when he'd made his little disclaimer. I was going to have to really focus and pay attention to this one when he spoke. No wandering in the corridors of my brain.

*That seems unlikely*, a voice called from one such long and dark hallway. That would be The Queen of the Zombies. I absolutely did not have time for her right this moment and put a mental seal on that particular part of my mind or whatever it is that I do to shut her up.

"So do you want to tell me why you are here and why you felt the need to speak in private?" Yay me for getting back on topic.

"The council has been made aware of your existence." That statement sounded like there was a meaning to it that I was not quite getting.

I decided to stay quiet and see if old Misty would speak some more on the subject. Instantly, I began to recollect this one girl I knew from my first or second waitressing job. Her name was Misty—

*Focus, Ava*, I barked at myself.

"Is it true that Morgan has not claimed you for her region?" Mystify was suddenly in Joe Friday-mode. I kept waiting for him to add, "Just the facts, ma'am."

He spun to face me directly. I felt something like a soft spongy needle was trying to poke inside my brain. I realize that a spongy needle might not make sense, but that is really the best way I can think to describe the feeling.

"What business is it of yours?" I answered. I noticed a slight tick at the corner of one eye on the man who now seemed even taller than when we first met. I had a mental flash of Gandalf towering over little Bilbo. That was a good physical description of Mystify except this version of Gandalf looked like he was no stranger to Botox.

"Kenny Rogers!" I blurted. That was who he really reminded me of; a seven foot tall version…and kind of skinny; but he had that face you could not get through nature. That had me wondering… "How old are you?"

"How are you doing this?" Mystify mumbled under his breath. I had a feeling I was not supposed to hear him and that he'd let that comment slip.

"Mystify!" the voice right behind me hissed, causing me to jump and spin with my claws extended and ready to shred whatever it was.

"Morgan?" I gasped, taking a step back and hiding my hands behind my back like a school boy with a straw and a handful of spitballs.

"Step back behind me, Ava."

Morgan's voice was as unemotional as always, but I could feel her anger coming off in hot waves. No, seriously…it was like being a foot away from a furnace. I glanced over at the tall man who now seemed frozen in place, then I moved back behind Morgan as she'd demanded. I was probably more surprised than she was that I had not argued or asked any questions.

"It seems that I owe you lunch," another voice called out. This one came from behind Mystify, but it was easily recognizable.

"Betty?"

I peeked over Morgan's shoulder as the older woman stepped out from behind a large tree that was just starting to show an abundance of lovely pale green leaves. The elderly looking woman busied her hands and produced a small glass object from inside her windbreaker.

"Ava," Betty said in a tone that sounded almost distracted as she focused on whatever it was that she had in her hands. Her eyes widened and she smiled big. "It seems that our friend here is alone."

"Pity," Morgan spoke as she stepped up to the man. Funny thing, she didn't sound at all like she meant it.

What happened next gave me the closest thing to a chill that I'd experienced in quite a while. A shimmering globe surrounded Mystify and I was immediately reminded of those Tesla balls they sell that have the lightning dancing around inside them…only different. The lightning did not come from the middle out, but exactly the opposite. And it all hit Mystify, lining him in an electric blue glow. I could see him screaming, but the globe obviously blocked all sound, because I did not hear a thing.

It lasted long enough that I began to wonder if this might just be a very lengthy torture. At last, the globe blinked out and the tall body fell in an awkward heap.

As a ghoul, I only eat the dead. A dead person has a smell that is irresistible and makes my mouth water just as yours might when you walk into a See's Candy store or Moonstruck Chocolate Café.

*Oh, and if you have not experienced Moonstruck, you have my pity.*

The thing is, up until that globe of light or energy or whatever it was disappeared, I had not been able to get even a hint of a smell from Mystify. Now? Well, that was a different story entirely.

For the first time in a while, Sharkmouth came into action without my bidding. The next thing I recall, I was sitting spread legged with my back against the base of a tree, a lumpy ball of regurgitated clothing was between my outstretched legs.

"What the hell was that?" I managed after a tremor rippled through me.

*You will suffer a thousand deaths for this, ghoul!* Mystify's voice railed. I looked around, expecting to see him standing right over me…then the realization came.

"You have got to be kidding," I moaned.

*I will see you stripped of your hide and allowed to regrow it a thousand times before I even consider the mercy of granting your death!*

"Oh hush, you'll do no such thing," I snapped. As quick as possible, I used the same methods I had learned—although "learned" is stretching it a bit—to isolate Adrianna.

"So it did work," Betty mused, alerting me to her presence about a dozen feet away. She and Morgan were perched on a limb about ten feet above the ground.

"What are you two doing up there?"

I realize that there were probably a thousand other questions that had more importance than that one, but I can't help what comes out of my mouth…*you should know that by now.* I watched as they drifted down like a pair of leaves. I could feel my annoyance building quickly. Once again, a whole lot of nothing was being said to the ghoul.

"You were not in control of your faculties," Betty answered after giving a sideways glance at Morgan.

"And why are you two here in Washington Park?" I asked.

"I received word about an hour ago that it was possible that there was an intruder in my district that might mean to do me harm," Morgan answered. "When I heard the description of this individual, I had little doubt who it was and what they might be after."

"Are you in trouble with your little Psychic Council?" I huffed as I got to my feet.

"Why would you think that?" Morgan asked with what was as close to amused as her voice was probably capable of sounding.

9

"Wasn't Stretch on the council?" I was dusting myself off and almost fell over when Morgan answered.

"No, why on earth would you think that?"

"Ummm…because he told me?" My voice ended a bit high which turned my statement into what sounded like a question.

"Mystify is the Dallas Psychic," Morgan replied.

"Texas or Oregon?" It seemed like a valid question to me.

"Texas of course." Morgan was back to her normal Spock-like self. Yet, I could swear I heard exasperation in her voice. "Now…what else did he tell you?"

I opened my mouth and just as quickly shut it with a snap and clash of teeth.

# 2

## I Want You to Want Me

Ghouls are not meant to travel great distances. We are supposedly guardians of our own specific territory. I guess one of Mother Nature's little tricks was in making us so sensitive to sunlight and lacking any sort of Supernatural ability in the speed department.

So, in order for me to be sitting in this Texas mansion, a lot had to occur. First, I was basically packaged up like a box of fine china. Hey, at least I had plenty of bubble wrap to play with during the flight. Now before you ask why I didn't just travel on a red eye flight—normally a four hour trip—consider all of the possibilities.

I hate that I just quoted Morgan, but basically those were her exact words to me when I asked about just hopping a late night flight when I was told that I would be going to Texas. The conversation went something like this:

"I think Alaska has a flight that goes straight through."

"And if there is any sort of delay that leaves you on the runway for a few hours? What will you do then? And can you ensure that every single passenger would be willing to accommodate your request to close the shutter on their window?

"Perhaps you feel comfortable going through the security check where they pat you down and might notice your abnor-

11

mally cool body temperature…or the fact that your eyes are solid black. You might be able to play the ruse of being blind…maybe. And then there is the color of your skin…airbrushing aside, which you would be doing by yourself now that Miss Jenkins is absent, any close examination would reveal flaws."

Morgan had a much higher opinion of the TSA's power of observation than I did. (And yes, I realize that comment probably earned me a spot on every strip search list, but since I will probably never be travelling anything but FedEx from now on…just consider my tongue firmly extended at you/them.)

The bad thing about bubble wrap is that it never lasts very long. So, after I had popped every single blister of plastic, I was left in the worst possible place I could imagine: alone with my thoughts. The other option was letting Adrianna and Mystify out of their little cubby holes that I'd stuffed them inside somewhere in my brain. Yeah, that was *not* an option.

So, I had nothing but time to think about the events of the past few weeks…mostly regarding Lisa's departure. I honestly thought that a day or two at the most would go by and she would come home. Nope. What made it worse was every single time I heard a knock at my door, I would bound to it like a puppy excited at the return of its master. Each time ended in disappointment. I probably bruised a few sets of feelings over the past several days.

Aoife probably took it the hardest. The last time she came over, the ritual of a knock at the door and me leaping to answer it ended with her running off into the darkness. The worst part of Supernatural hearing is how long I heard her crying well after she vanished from sight.

As I sat in the giant crate and sunk into an even deeper depression that not even Candy Crush could distract me from, I tried to piece together everything that I knew for certain when it came to me, Lisa, Templars, and the whole Supernatural biz. It was about an hour when the revelation hit. I didn't know a damn thing!

Now for many, that is not a big surprise. In fact, I know of several individuals who make it a regular point to draw attention to that fact. When I got home, I would have to make it a point to hunt Lisa down—for lack of a better term—and beg her to accept my apology. I had been an idiot.

I felt us land and realized that somewhere along the trip, a coat of frost had built up on my skin. The freezing temperatures had not even registered. That was something to keep in mind.

The unloading and transporting of my crate to a moving van had me regretting my earlier fun with the bubble wrap. I would have to give the folks at FedEx a call about how a package marked 'Fragile' was treated.

At long last, my trip ended with my delivery to the very mansion of which I am currently a 'guest' resident. Since it was still dark when I arrived, I was given a brief tour by a vampire that might have an even worse attitude than Belinda. That had me wondering what it was about Psychics and vampires.

"Claude will see you shortly," Bitch-with-fangs muttered before leaving me alone in a room with more books than most libraries.

*Claude?* I thought. Not a very cool name like Morgan or Mystify. After an hour, I wondered if long lifespans make vampires lose the meaning of words like "soon" or "shortly." I was just about to go and see if I could find the mysterious Claude when the door to the library opened and a man walked in.

*There is no way that is Claude*, was the first thought that came to mind. If Vince Neil of Mötley Crüe in his prime had a twin, it was this guy.

"You must be Ava Birch," the man said in a voice that was like audible sex. I mean, he had that rough tone with just a bit of a rasp, and he spoke not quite in a whisper, but I found myself leaning forward as if to hear him better out of some sort of reflex; which is weird considering my Supernatural hearing.

"Cl-Cl-Claude?" I stammered.

"Yes, and how rude of me for not making that clear right away."

*Oooo, he's a smooth one*, Adrianna cooed from the back of my brain. Mystify was strangely silent considering the fact that

I'd become so distracted that I had completely dropped all my mental compartments.

*Don't let him fool you, Miss Birch, he is a stone cold killer*, the voice of Mystify finally sang out.

"So you are the new Psychic of Dallas," I stated, keeping Mystify's statement on file for future reference.

"I am now," Claude said with a smile. "And I believe that I have you to thank for that."

"Unfortunately," I grumped.

I still was not too keen on being a killer. And it had all happened so fast. Plus, I could hardly take all the credit; Morgan and maybe even Betty had a hand in that whole situation.

"And now you have come here...?" he ended on what was obviously a question.

"To find out what you wanted. You are not part of the council as you led Mystify to believe, and neither is he. I find all of this interesting since Psychics are great at not telling the entire truth, but I did not know they were such consummate liars."

(*Yep, still got my word-of-the-day calendar...bet you forgot, huh?*)

"Miss Birch..." Claude eased himself down into a great big chair with red velvet padding. I almost expected him to produce a great big book and start reading me a story. "Times are changing in a manner that the Supernatural community might not be prepared to deal with as need be. It is essential that only those capable of handling this oncoming threat be in positions of authority."

"Okay, I'll bite...what is the newest threat on the horizon?"

Seriously, this would not be a very entertaining book series if there was not some long arcing storyline mixed in with the little adventures, right? I mean, if you watched *Buffy the Vampire Slayer*, you had the fun little stand-alone episodes, but there was still some season-long drama that had to be resolved in the epic finale, right? My favorite was when Willow went evil and started stripping the skin from guys. So cool.

"Why...the Templars, of course," Claude said with a frown. "Has Morgan told you nothing?"

14

I felt a tingle in my brain that was totally new. Somehow, I was aware that Claude was not being entirely truthful.

*That would be me*, Mystify's voice whispered in my mind. *As I told you, be careful of this one.*

"Maybe you can fill me in."

I hoped that it was not looking like I was hearing voices in my head. After all, Morgan had been very aware of my ability to absorb some of the powers of those I consumed if they happened to be Supernatural. I had Adrianna's ability to talk with and supposedly even animate the dead. Now it seemed that I might have a little insight as to the abilities and nature of a Psychic.

I looked around and found a chair, since it was obvious that my host lacked the manners to offer me one. Once I was comfy, I folded my hands in my lap and nodded for him to continue. It would be really cool if he had no idea that he was in the presence of a real life polygraph…only, unlike those stupid machines, my ability to discern truth was actually real and not some sort of electronic voodoo.

"The Templars have been building their strength and numbers for eons. They have perfected the crafting of weapons which mean true death to *almost* every Supernatural known."

I noticed his emphasis on the word "almost" during his little introduction to what sounded like it was going to be another case of a Psychic talking to me like I was Ava the Idiot Child. I decided to be a touch on the proactive side and hopefully show him that, while I may not know everything, I was far from stupid.

"Old news, Claude. And having seen Blue Steel weaponry in action, I can understand the concern of the Supernatural community…kind of like the rest of the world after the United States dropped that first atomic bomb. But none of this means diddly squat. Why did you come to Texas and send Mystify to his death?"

"Isn't it obvious?"

My head rattled as both Claude and Mystify posed the same question at the exact same time.

I slumped in my chair. Okay, maybe I was Ava the Idiot Child.

"So that you would come here. I knew that Morgan would send you if you did in fact exist. And if the rumors were true, which, according to my powers of detection, they are, you have not been claimed. I would have you as my own, Ava Birch."

I can't be certain, but I think I felt Mystify's jaw drop even wider than mine. I took a few seconds to recover. I might have even reached up manually to give my chin a nudge that shut my gaping mouth. This would be the second Psychic to come at me with an offer of claiming me. The first one had offered me an army. I could not wait to see what Claude here had in mind.

"And why should I leave all that I know to come here?" I asked once I found my words.

"First, it is obvious that you are not being properly utilized. If that were not the case, there is no way that you could not be more aware of what is happening with the Templars. I would not keep you in the dark. How can a weapon so powerful be wielded adequately if kept in its case? And, my pet, that is exactly what is happening to you."

Okay, I may not be a super liberated type of woman. I admit that I liked it when a guy opened a door for me or pulled my chair out at a restaurant. However, old Claude here and I were not on nickname status. I was nobody's *pet*, and the way he said that word…he meant it; and not in a good way.

"Ahh…" Claude leaned back and folded his hands in his lap with a scowl. "I see that I have offended you."

Umm…was I that obvious? I mean, sure…he had tweaked my agitation knob just a bit with that "pet" thing, but since when did a Psychic care one tiny bit about annoying the lowly ghoul? Perhaps I could at least give this guy a listen.

"I am not a pet. If you want to think of a cutesy nickname, try sugar lumps or love dumplin' next time. I just did not care for the way you called me your *pet*. It sounded too…ownery."

He frowned, but I think it was at my made up word. He had a certain air about him that screamed yuppie. If this were the 80s, he would be wearing a polo shirt with a sweater tied loosely at the neck. Basically, he would be one of the country club snobs from *Trading Places* who turn their back on Dan Aykroyd when

16

he gets set up by those greedy Duke Brothers.

"I apologize."

Those two words actually hit me pretty hard. I was almost certain that Morgan would have as much trouble saying that she was sorry as Fonzie did trying to say he was wrong. I was now completely off balance.

*Looking back, I am pretty sure that was the desired effect. What better way to get somebody to forget any type of common sense than to absolutely disorient them so that they can't tell up from down?*

"Yeah…well…don't let it happen again." I gave him a coy flip of my left hand like it was no big deal. The thing is, there was a voice in my head screaming a warning…literally.

*Ava, snap out of it. You can't possibly be falling for this nonsense*, Adrianna was scolding.

*Are you really this daft, woman?* Mystify railed from some dark corner of my brain despite my best efforts to silence them both.

It actually took me longer than it should have to silence them and lock them back up where they belonged. Something was messing with my abilities to box off parts of my mind. Like a silly cow, I just chalked it up to still not being in total control of my new powers.

"So, perhaps we can discuss in greater detail what it might take to convince you to move here and join my ser—" Claude paused; it was so brief I almost missed it. Instead, all I missed was another clue. "You can become part of the family here. Truthfully, our Supernatural community would flourish with the addition of one such as yourself."

There was something in his eyes that briefly reminded me of what a mean cartoon spider would look like in human form, but just as quickly, it was replaced with such warmth that it made me all tingly.

He'd said the magic word: family.

I don't like to talk about it much, but I never had one of those close families like you saw on *Family Ties* or *The Cosby Show*. Heck, I would have settled for *Roseanne*; at least it was obvious when all the chips were down that they loved each other. My home was just the place where everybody eventually came to sleep.

I imagine that was why I jumped into my one and only failed marriage so quickly. I think I just wanted to try and create what I'd always imagined a family to be. Who knew I would never be able to get pregnant? If I'd been able to, perhaps I could have kept my marriage together.

WHOA!

Okay, I am used to having my mind go on little field trips to Ava Land. In fact, it turns out that is one of my powers…sort of. However, I am not used to those trips being so dreary. I am not one of those people who moans that my childhood is the reason for every bit of grief that comes my way as an adult, nor is every personality flaw able to be blamed on some childhood tragedy. So why am I sailing down the River of Self-Pity? That is SO not me.

"…and you would of course have plenty of assistants to take care of the menial tasks like ensuring your freezer is stocked with fresh corpses."

Hmm, I see I still tend to miss out on the important stuff whether my mind is in happy Ava Land or the sad version. While I'd been in my little pit of sadness, Claude had led me to a huge dining room with one of those ridiculously long tables where you practically have to shout to be heard by the person at the far end.

I tripped as my eyes came to rest on what I had originally thought to be a decorative center piece. I walked up to the table and took a closer look. I glanced over my shoulder at Claude who was steepling his fingers like Mr. Burns from *The Simpsons* and giving me a smile that should be comforting or encouraging but only provided me with a chill.

Laid out on the table was what I can only describe as a Brett Michaels clone. He was decked out in the fashionably ripped stonewash jeans and a tight black tee. He had animal print scarves in all the right spots and even sported a gold threaded black bandanna that kept his perfect peroxide blonde hair out of his eyes that I just knew would be a dazzling sexy blue.

"I have taken the liberty of preparing your meal. I believe you should find it to your liking," Claude's voice was rattling around in my head, but all I could do was stare with open-mouthed amazement.

He was so perfect and beautiful. And it was not the *Rock of Love* Brett...nay, nay, Moose Breath. This was *Look What the Cat Dragged In* Brett at his skinny, delicious best.

The next few minutes went by in a blur as Sharkmouth came on and the Brett clone vanished like a roll of raw cookie dough at a Sad Girl convention. The thing is, after I was done, I had the hollowest feeling. The best thing that I can compare it to is if you ever buy that Krab meat; for one, it doesn't even really taste a thing like crab. And yeah, I spelled it with a "K" on purpose just like they do on the package. You see, it is not real crab, but rather some sort of white fish that they pumped with (and this really kills me...even though I am already technically dead) *imitation* crab flavoring. So what better way to make fake crab than to make it with fake crab flavor.

I'd just eaten a dead guy that looked like Brett, but as soon as I finished, my brain was already taunting me about how it wasn't the real thing. Of course that might have just been Adrianna.

In any case, when I looked up, I realized that Claude and I were no longer alone. A group of three vampires stood at his left shoulder and a big hairy thing towered on his right. I have no idea how I'd finished my meal with the wretched stench that now filled the room. These vampires all reeked unlike any I'd ever known. Then I realized that they were different in more ways than just their odor. These things did not have the intelligence and emotionless evil like Belinda and her kin.

"Revenants?" I blurted. "And just what is that?" I sniffed in the direction of the wet wookie, but could not really pick up anything.

"The revenants are quite tame I can assure you."

*Says the man with the pet great white shark*, I thought. I heard a snicker, but I wasn't sure if it was Adrianna or Mystify.

19

"As for this poor misunderstood creature—"

It let out a series of guttural noises that actually sounded a great deal like the hairy beast made famous in the *Star Wars* movies. My mind tried to go to another dark memory…that horrific *Star Wars Christmas Special* with special guests Bea Arthur and Harvey Korman. I shook it off.

"…is known as a Swamp Ape. The best I can relate it to you would be something akin to your Pacific Northwest Bigfoot."

"Uh-huh." Seriously, what else was I going to say to that?

"I wanted you to see just what you would have at your disposal." Claude did this open armed gesture like he was Monty Hall showing me what I'd just won behind curtain number two. He was acting like I'd just hit the Big Deal of the Day, but I was feeling like I'd scored the klunker.

"Half-crazed vampires and the soggy Sasquatch?" I made no effort to hide how completely unimpressed I was at that moment.

"As a ghoul, it is important that you have shock troops when the big threat rears its head, and trust me when I tell you that this Templar situation is as big as it gets to our kind."

I was just not feeling the gratitude. I mean, at home, I had a siren, a pair of jötunn, who knows how many goblins, and a contingent of bugbears (which are basically nine foot tall mogwai on steroids with a mouth full of teeth that rival my Sharkmouth). And the best thing about them is that they didn't belong to anybody. They *chose* to follow me!

A feeling crashed into me like a case of Montezuma's Revenge. The thought was that these individuals who had decided to follow me could just as easily decide to leave the moment that things get bad. After all, that was sort of what had happened with Lisa.

Wait. That wasn't entirely accurate. Lisa had not actually walked out on me as much as I'd pushed her away. That thought only added fuel to the fire as my mind ticked off a number of scenarios where I did basically the exact same thing with all my new little minions. After all, hadn't I recently hurt that sweet little siren Aoife's feelings?

## I Want You to Want Me

Where was all this Debbie Downer crap coming from? On cue, Adrianna and Mystify both started to yell at me, but it was as if they were too far away, and I could not exactly hear them.

Next, on a Very Special *That Ghoul Ava…*

# 3

# Dead Man's Party

"Perhaps you would care to take a while and get yourself together. You seem a bit disheveled," Claude offered. He was standing over me, but I must have been spacing out more than usual because I had no recollection of him ever having gotten up and crossed the room.

"Huh?" I shook my head and immediately wondered why people did that and actually thought that the act of shaking their brain around in the skull would bring some sort of clarity.

"You have had a rough journey. I can't imagine what it must be like to be forced to travel like so much baggage. Well, rest assured, if you come to work for me, I will ensure that you have a private jet so that there are no more instances like that in your life."

*Private jet?* I thought. Wow, I was just getting used to having my sweet Corvette and a nice house; which was already for sale as I had been forced to move out into the country because of all my new additions. Seriously, there really was no way to have a pair of giants walking around the yard without attracting attention. Even if they are just kids.

I felt like I was in a dream. One of those disgusting revenants skittered over to me and made a gesture with her head that indicated I should follow. Since my flight out of here was not for three days (a number decided by Morgan and Betty after a long conversation that I was pretty much excluded from), I had nothing else to do. Also, I glanced at my watch and realized that the sun would be coming up soon.

The revenant led me down a flight of stairs and to a long hallway with doors lining both sides. It gave a motion with its arms that basically told me I could just go check things out on my own. In a flash, the revenant was gone.

I really did not know what was expected of me, so I went to the first door and opened it. I had no idea what I thought I would find; part of me figured it might be like the faerie sidhe complex. I would open the door to an impossibly large room that could only be an extension into some other dimension or whatever it was that governed the laws of space in a faerie lair.

"Welcome, Miss Birch," a rough voice that reminded me of gravel being dumped into a cast iron skillet announced.

I cocked my head to one side and tried to figure out what it was that I was looking at. All I was certain of was that it was female. It had two rows of breasts; four per side. The head was almost like a pig…or maybe I mean boar. It had two big teeth jutting up from the lower jaw. The ears were elongated and pointy, poking up from tufts of coarse, black hair.

"Okay…I give." I gave a slight shrug of the shoulders.

"Mud troll," she replied after making a sound with her mouth that might have been a laugh, but instead, sounded more like horse flatulence.

"Okay, how many sorts of trolls are there?" It seemed like a logical question, and I might as well learn something while I'm here talking to a mud troll.

I stepped inside and was surprised that this room was actually quite normal and did not appear to be connected to some other plane of existence. However, there was a muggy sort of warmth in the air that I did not find appealing. My hair would be destroyed if I hung out in here too long.

"How many types of humans are there?" the mud troll replied.

I was not sure what she meant. I mean, when it came down

to it, there was really only one sort. A human was a human. Now, did she mean that in ethnicity, gender...or some other classification of which I was not aware?

After I stood there with what I am pretty certain was a dumbfounded look on my face for a few seconds, she made an even more obscene sounding noise that I was just going to have to assume to be laughter.

"Much like humans are proud of their heritage, be it Asian, Spanish, or German, trolls have similar divisions based on the environment that they feel most comfortable."

"Okay, and are there such drastic variations in size?" I was remembering the giant lake troll that had popped up out the water in Tillamook and ate a handful of human-sized faeries like they were Skittles.

"Our size is predicated on our eating habits. Some trolls feel the need to gorge themselves and thus undergo transformation to what you would consider giant. The drawback is the need to continue to maintain that sort of consumption. Long ago, it might have been much simpler, but with humans spread across the globe like locusts, it is difficult for a troll to find a lair that would not eventually be discovered."

That seemed like a logical answer. I gave a polite nod.

"So you are here as a *guest* of the new Psychic." It wasn't a question, and the word 'guest' did not sound exactly right.

"Yep," I answered.

*Ask Gretch if she misses the old one*, Mystify called out. I could hear something in his voice that was probably sadness. That meant he had presided over this mud troll—or whatever you call it that Psychics do in regards to their district.

"And how is this new Psychic working out for you?" I tried to sound casual. I had no idea if this thing knew that I had her old Psychic bouncing around in my head or not.

"No idea," Gretch said with what I was certain had to be a sigh. "He has not gotten down this far yet to visit with the lessers. I imagine he will get down to it eventually, considering the rumors that he is building an army."

*He hasn't even bothered to come down here! And why is*

*Gretch here in the first place?* It felt like Mystify was in the front of my brain…and trying to get out through my left eye.

"Just settle down," I snapped as I dug the heel of my hand into my eye like it would stop the sudden outburst.

"Excuse me?" Gretch tilted her head at me in question.

"Sorry, I didn't mean you." I waved a hand in her direction and then focused my inner voice. *Just settle down, Mystify. I honestly don't think your presence in my head is something that anybody except Betty and Morgan are actually aware of, let's keep it that way. If you have questions or comments, then give them, but you need to stay where I put you.*

*And you will notice that there is a lot of room,* Adrianna snarked.

*You know, if I find a way to eat you a second time so that you are gone for good…* I let that just hang there. Funny thing, I could feel Adrianna shrink back. Maybe I could do such a thing. Hmm…I might have to look into that.

"…just seemed so angry, and the last thing I want to do is anger one such as yourself," Gretch was babbling. Even worse, she had dropped to her knees.

"Okay," I said in as gentle of a voice as I could muster, "let's get up off the floor." I crossed the room and offered my hand to the shivering mud troll.

"P-p-please don't eat me." Gretch threw her hands over her head.

"First, I am not going to eat you, and second…" Hey, what do you know, I didn't really have a second. "Well, I'm still not going to eat you."

The mud troll's face turned up at me, and I could see dark stains running down it. She had been crying. For the love of Pete, what the hell kind of reputation did ghouls have? I was going to need to get my hands on that *Unnatural Grimoire*. If anything could tell me about ghouls and the powers that we possess, I bet it was in that book.

Gretch rose to her feet, but she was still all closed in on herself, obviously terrified. I needed to change that as soon as possible. I decided to dig out my old waitress charm and dust it off.

"Here," I guided her to a chair and eased her into it, "have a seat and maybe you can tell me a little about yourself. For one, how did you come to be here?" I felt Mystify's attention really sharpen. I had a feeling he was interested in the answer—perhaps even more than I was.

"I was what humans would call a rescue troll." Gretch wiped her eyes and looked down at her lap. "My family perished in a terrible storm and I was living down on the banks of the river that they call the Rio Grande. I didn't know any better…and crossed in to goblin territory.

"Of course they captured me and brought me back to their warren. I would have been in the stew pot that night—"

*Except I was meeting with the goblin king that day*, Mystify said just as Gretch was saying basically the same thing.

"I had never seen a human up close before. My parents had told me all the stories about how horrible they are, how they are a violent and murderous creature. So, when this man came up to me as I was being led to the stew pot…I screamed."

"Wait!" I held up my hands to keep her from continuing. I had to get something clear. "You were about to be dropped in a stew pot. You were going to become mud troll bisque, but you did not scream until you ran in to what you assumed to just be a normal human?"

Gretch nodded like everything I said made perfect sense. She was not seeing the problem with the whole "about to be boiled and ladled into a bowl" thing.

"This is the way of things," she said simply.

I've been told by a few of the Supernaturals that I have the problem of seeing the world through human eyes. I had to assume this was just another of those moments. I gave her a gesture with my hand to continue her story.

"Anyways, this human stepped forward and demanded that the goblins release me. Of course that meant that I was now his to command."

*Well of course it does*, I thought. However, I could sense Adrianna and Mystify both finding amusement in my lack of knowledge when it comes to the customs of my new community.

"I was bundled up and brought here. Of course I was prepared for the most terrible death—"

"And that would be something worse than being boiled alive and eaten," I scoffed.

"Of course. At least my death would have purpose in granting strength and sustenance to another. Now I thought I would simply be killed and discarded. That is what humans do, is it not?"

"Unless you're made of bacon," I mumbled. Gretch gave me a funny look. I just sighed and bid her continue with her tale.

"So he gave me a room in his home and soon began to teach me the things that my parents had not had time to do yet when it came to the ways of mud trolls. He showed me my powers."

She said that last bit with a sniff. I could tell that she was recalling some wonderful childhood memories. I was curious as to what sorts of "powers" a mud troll might have, but Mystify was begging for my attention.

*Ask her why she is down here, this is the holding cells. She has a room in the house and always has.*

"So what are you doing down here? Don't you have a room in the regular part of the—" I felt my mouth snap shut suddenly. "Wait, these are the holding cells?"

"Yes."

Such a small word, but I swear I heard a sound cue like a prison cell door sliding home and slamming shut with a metallic clang. Now, to be honest, I have never been to jail or anything of that sort. The closest I came was the holding room at the local Fred Meyer's when I pocketed a lip gloss. I was twelve and the whole "call your parents" thing was not nearly as scary as the greasy bum they brought in about ten minutes later and cuffed to another chair across the room. For some reason, my mind made the connection that if I ever did this again, I would be like that smelly man with the molding food in his bird's nest of a beard. I still shudder when I remember his brown and yellow-toothed grin with the four or five gaping black holes where a tooth was supposed to be.

I turned on my heel and walked back out to the corridor. Glancing both ways, I suddenly realized how dank and empty this place was. Maybe it was just my mind playing tricks, but it was as if I was seeing this place for the first time. It was almost stereotypical in the dankness and gloominess.

I stomped to the stairs and climbed them with my anger growing at each step. The door was one of those heavy oaken monstrosities with the huge iron hinges and even a big twisted ring for a door knob.

"Don't open that—" Gretch was calling a warning, but it was too late.

I flung the door open and shrieked as fire engulfed me from head to toe. I was able to slam the door shut, but I think it was more instinctive than anything else. In the whole mess, I had obviously used my ghoulish leaping skills to fling myself back down the stairs.

I lay on the cold stone, wishing for its chill to seep into my skin and cool the horrible burning sensation that had brought on my switchdigits (yep, fingers and toes) as well as Sharkmouth. I was back to being a novice with no control over my powers…or at least that was how it seemed at the moment. I mean, that was twice with the Sharkmouth in less than an hour.

"That doorway faces a large open window. The master leaves the curtains open to keep the exit bathed in sunlight by day," Gretch said as she knelt beside me.

*I told you to watch this guy*, Mystic snarled. *For one, I never put any of my citizens down here. This place was only for those who came in to my territory unannounced.*

*How does it feel to be the one who is locked up?* Adrianna scoffed. *Not so much fun, is it?*

"You better pray I can't find a way to eat you twice," I growled.

Gretch bowed her head. "If that is your will."

*Huh? Wait!* Crap, I'd said that last bit out loud. I was really going to have to watch that. If I did it at a more inopportune time, I might tip my hand to somebody who knows the specifics on ghouls.

"No, not you," I managed through clenched teeth as waves of flame rolled over me. Maybe not for real, but that is exactly what it felt like at the moment.

"What is all the ruckus!" a voice shouted.

I swear it was the Wilford Brimley guy from the Quaker Oats and (as of late) diabetes commercial. And here is a question…is it pronounced dye-a-bee-tees, or is it dia-bee-tus. I never know. And is one version the plural of another?

"…opened the door," Gretch was explaining.

I glanced up to see what I can only describe as a cross between Woodsy the Owl and Smokey the Bear. It was about ten feet tall, walking on hind…claws…and covered with a thick brown fur that had a smattering of feathers until it reached the shoulders where the feathers sort of took over. It had big paws at the end of what I am just going to call its arms since it was walking upright. But looking down on me were teacup saucer-sized eyes that were peering out from an owl's face. I really hoped that my gray skin did not make me look like a mouse.

"…do a fool thing like that, don't she have a lick a sense?" Wilford the Owl was scolding.

And then it suddenly seemed to really get a look at me. You would have thought that he was the one sprawled on the floor being towered over by a giant…*thing*.

"What the hell are you?" I managed. Probably could have asked with more tact, but to do so would have meant that I was focusing on the here and now, which I was absolutely not. My little mind wanderings turned out to be a ghoulish trait. I can just slip away into my mind and ignore things like pain…or instructions from Morgan.

"My name is Theodore, and as for your actual question, I am an owlbear."

*Not very original*, I thought.

"And beggin' the lady's pardon, I had no idea that you were a ghoul. Please, if I am to be dispatched, I only ask that you allow me to finish my book. I am so near the end, it would be a shame not to—"

"What are you babbling about," I hissed as I tried to sit up.

"I have angered you. You are a ghoul. Using simple logic, my life is forfeit," Theodore the Owlbear said, ruffling his neck feathers in obvious fear.

I really needed to do some research on ghouls. Every Supernatural that I was meeting seemed to see me as a cross between Charles Manson and Attila the Hun. Basically, I was the boogeyman...or woman as the case may be.

"I'm not going to eat you." I sat up and felt the pain creeping back to the edges of my awareness.

Looking around, I saw several of the doors along this corridor were now open. The faces peering out were enough to send a child screaming in horror. Fortunately for me, I had seen my share of beasties. From the looks of it, there were a bunch of goblins and a few bugbears. The only new creatures turned out to be the mud troll and the owlbear...so far at least.

"So...the Psychic has sent a ghoul to do his dirty work!" a small voice barked.

I was not in the least bit surprised to see a goblin strut out into the center of the hallway. From my experience, goblins were basically fearless; not very bright, though.

"I'm not here to do anybody's dirty work," I said through clenched teeth. I was losing my footing in Ava Land and the pain was starting to get to me.

"Wrinkle Butt!" Gretch stood and turned to face the goblin that had now closed the distance between us by half.

And just like that, the pain receded a little. *What is it with goblin names?* I wondered. So far, I'd met a Nose Wart, Sour Nipple, Stinky Tongue, and now Wrinkle Butt. It was like a twisted version of Mad Libs.

"Go and fetch one of the zombies!" Gretch ordered.

Just like that, Adrianna perked up. I could feel her trying to find a way out of the most recent box that I'd placed her in towards the back of my mind.

"Wait...you have zombies?" I asked.

I was not entirely sure, but from what I'd learned in my little adventure with the aforementioned Adrianna, zombies were created magically. I know that had been a real disappointment to

Lisa. She had held on to some twisted and perverse hope that one of her favorite book, television, and movie subjects could actually come to being. I did not see the thrill of a world wiped out to the point of near human extinction. Granted, it would be a walking buffet for me, however, I had a feeling there would be a lot fewer "Ricks" in the world and a lot more "Governors" if you get what I'm trying to say.

I missed whatever exchange took place between Gretch and Wrinkle Butt, and I know this because my next moment of clarity was when the most delicious smell hit me. I came out of my reverie to discover a woman standing before me. She was in pretty bad shape and looked like all I would have to do was touch her and she would fall apart. This was definitely no movie zombie; this was the real deal in all its rotten glory. Basically...

DELICIOUS!

And then I was sitting in the hallway all by myself. Somewhere along the way, everybody had run off to their rooms. At least that was what it looked like. Not even Gretch remained. However, I'd lost my containment of both Mystify and Adrianna.

I was just about to lock them both away when Adrianna practically cried. She was begging and pleading in a way that was very much not like her usual bitchy self.

*If there are zombies, somebody had to create them*, she said hurriedly, knowing that she could not waste time with banter since I was obviously so tired of her already.

I was not sure if her being in my mind made her privy to just how serious I was about finding a way to be rid of her for good. Whatever the case, she was all business at the moment in a way that I'd not ever seen from her.

*That troll creature said the word in its plural form...she said for that goblin to go and fetch* one *of the zombies.*

*So?* I concentrated on keeping this conversation internal. I was going to have to get better at that if I had any chance at keeping it a secret; and something told me that was very important right about now.

*If there are more than one, I might be able to identify the creator*, Adrianna insisted.

*Why does that even matter?* I was obviously missing something.

*Think about it, Ava,* Adrianna said, although not in a nasty way. She was actually trying to be helpful, or so it seemed. *If Morgan sent you after me because I was considered such a huge threat, don't you think that this might be equally important?*

*Yes, but you were trying to wipe out the world...create an army of undead. The last time you did that, you wiped out a third of the population of the European continent.*

Oh yeah, I'd done my homework on the Black Plague after that whole ordeal. Part of it had been simple curiosity. I had discovered that she was sort of a celebrity among the Supernatural world.

*That is beside the point*, Adrianna insisted. I think we would have to agree to disagree on that subject. However, she was not finished pleading her case. *You know how humans have that odd tendency to commit what are eventually called copycat killings? Well, there have been a few necromantic pretenders over the years who have tried to recreate my work. If this Claude has discovered one, and if that person has been successful in any way, there could be trouble for your precious human race.*

I considered her words. There had in fact been an actual zombie, of that there could be no doubt. Granted, it looked horrible, but it was still able to walk. That was at least a start.

*Okay, so if I take you to these zombies...what will you be able to figure out?*

Adrianna was silent again, and I could tell that she was really trying to think of something. When she spoke, she confirmed my suspicions.

*Listen, Ava, I don't want to offend you, so the best way I can think to describe this is that magic is very personal. Each person who wields it must draw on some of their own inner spark. That leaves what you might call a watermark. Nobody can do magic without leaving a trace of the originator. Normally, that would not matter. However, if I can get a read on this particular person's magic, then I would be able to identify that individual should you happen to encounter them at some point.*

It sounded reasonable. Of course I quickly went through all of the possible ways that this could go wrong. When none of them seemed too catastrophic, I agreed. That was when I got my first surprise. Adrianna taught me how to tune myself to a zombie. My sense would now ignore anything dead or living. All I would sense was a zombie. It is way cooler than it probably sounds.

I went to the end of the hallway and stopped at a door that looked like all the rest. It was not until that moment that I realized my normal ghoulish super senses had not been really doing me any good down here. I'd had to go and open that first door to discover Gretch. Why hadn't I realized that earlier? Oh well, nothing could be done about it at the moment.

I opened the door. Honestly, I had no idea what to expect. Nothing could have prepared me for what I walked in to.

The room was huge. In fact, if I had to guess, I would say that it was a giant U in shape. I was willing to bet that it wrapped all the way around to the door that was at my back and across the hall. There was only one piece of furniture…a giant bed. Sprawled on that bed was a man. Here is where it gets weird.

The man was absolutely naked. All around him were more zombies. You probably guessed, but if you didn't, I can confirm to you that they were all female. And yes…all naked. There was a mirror ball hanging from the ceiling and a red spotlight was hitting it to shower the room in crimson twinkles that whirled about slowly.

It took me a moment to recognize the song that was playing. *Pretty in Pink* by the Psychedelic Furs. And I swear…the zombies were swaying to the music!

*What in the world?*

Yeah, even Adrianna was blown away. I was so mesmerized that I hadn't even gone in to Sharkmouth mode. I have no idea how long I just stood there in disbelief, but at some point, the song had changed. It was some 80s synth piece that I did not recognize, and I only say 80s synth piece because it had that very specific sound like something from a *Miami Vice* episode.

"Excuse me?" I had finally had enough of just standing there and being ignored.

The man looked up, but he did not look in the least bit surprised, annoyed, or (and this is the one I was expecting) embarrassed. He slid out from between a pair of female zombies and scootched to the end of the bed, sliding his feet in to a pair of slippers.

Seriously? I mean, this guy is buck ass naked, and he puts on slippers? Not a robe or even a pair of boxers? And can I just go on the record again as saying that, boys, your stuff is nothing to be flaunting. It really is not a very attractive piece of your body. Yes, I agree that it can have its uses when wielded properly, but when the little soldier is at parade rest...its just icky looking. And even worse for this guy...*he* of the uncircumcised. Now it just looked like a very depressed and miniature aardvark.

"Far out!" The guy sounded almost exactly like Jeff Spicoli from *Fast Times at Ridgemont High*.

And it was just that quick. All my senses seemed to return in a flood. I could smell everything in this room. This guy was baked!

*You have got to be kidding*, Adrianna said with even more disbelief than I felt.

"Hey," Stoner Boy said with far too much glee in his voice, "are you real? I mean, you don't look like one of my babes...but you got a funky vibe going on that I can't get my mind to wrap around."

"First, I am quite real. My name is Ava Birch, and I am a ghoul."

"A what?" He sounded confused, but definitely not afraid.

"You mind telling me what is going on down here?" I asked. I was not going to waste time trying to explain myself to this guy.

"You the cops?" Oh, sure, now he sounded a bit nervous.

"No, I am not the police."

"Because you gotta tell me if I ask...I know my rights, man...err...woman...ma'am." Now he was just blabbering.

"I can assure you that I am not in any way tied to a law enforcement agency of any type. Okay?" He nodded. "Now, can you tell me your name?"

"Cody…Cody Ryan."

"Okay, Cody, and as I said, my name is Ava Birch."

I waited a moment to see if anything would register in his eyes like coherence, but I gave up on that front after a while. Seriously, the young man had some major issues that I doubted a gallon of Visine could handle.

"So…maybe you can tell me what is going on here." I walked in to the room and shut the door behind me. I did not really want anybody eavesdropping.

"Just making my army of fembots," Cody said with a Cheshire grin.

He reached over and ran his fingers through the pale blonde strands of one of the zombies standing beside him. I had to bite back a shudder when most of the hair…and a good piece of scalp came away with his hand. How was he not seeing that?

"Fembots?" I looked around the room. That was when I noticed that all of these girls were blonde, and for some reason, they were just standing around. They had taken no notice of me at all.

*That's because you are not a living, warm-blooded person,* Adrianna informed me.

"Like in Aush-tin Powersh, bay-bee."

He needed help on his impersonation. He just sounded like Spicoli with a speech impediment. I'd never known the use of marijuana to cause slurring.

"Uh-huh. So how 'bout you show me how you make your Fembots," I urged.

"No can do, sweets."

I forced back the desire to slap this idiot. I was anything but sweet. Also, I was guessing this kid to be no older than twenty…and that was pushing it.

*Maybe if you try to sweet talk him,* Mystify suggested.

*I take it you don't recognize this young man?* I asked.

*He is new…and I can also assure you that, at no time did I ever allow revenants to have free run of my home.*

"C'mon," I tried to sound flirty, but I was afraid it just came off as creepy.

*If you could get him to do this, I would have a good idea of what you might be dealing with*, Adrianna added.

"What can you offer for trade?" Cody flopped back down on his bed...literally.

"Trade?"

"Yeah...the guy that runs this place has hooked me up with these sweet digs as well as all the ganja I want...what do you have?"

"Well..." I was stumped. I didn't have anything.

"Strip," Cody leered.

Next, on a Very Special *That Ghoul Ava…*

# Strip

"What?" Adrianna, Mystify and I said simultaneously.

"You got a pretty decent bod for an older lady...and this weed must really be awesome, because your tan looks gray. I ain't got no ones, so if you strip, my tip will be that I make a Fembot and let you watch."

"*Older* lady?" I coughed.

"You gotta be at least thirty..."

I never cease to be amazed at the human male. I swear, especially in the younger ones, there is nothing that a girl could not obtain if she flashes a bit of skin. All you need to do is find out if they are a boob man or a butt man. That is truly the only mystery to unlocking the secrets of any male mind. The problem is that, once you manage to open that little treasure chest, you too often discover that it is empty.

"So why would you want to see me strip?"

"Because I'm bored."

Talk about making a girl feel special.

"And if I do this, you'll make a Fembot?"

*You can't possibly be serious*, Adrianna and Mystify said in unison. I ignored them.

"That's the deal."

Well...at least he hadn't asked for me to have sex with him.

And besides, it wasn't like I hadn't done this before. Oh…you didn't know about that? Well, maybe someday I'll clue you in on that little chapter of my life. Trust me…it is far from glamorous.

"Do I get to pick the song or do you?"

That caught him off guard. I think he had expected me to balk at his offer.

"You go ahead."

"Okay, where is your iPod?"

Music had been playing this entire time, so he had to have some sort of music player down here. Sure enough, he pointed to an iPod sitting in the lap of one of the zombie/Fembots that was seated on one side of his bed. I did not want to think of why it would be there of all places.

I picked up the device and thumbed the wheel around until I found his music. If possible, this kid was an even bigger fan of 80s music than I was. As for the choice…it was too easy.

The sound of the motorcycles being kick started came through the still hidden speakers. *Girls, Girls, Girls!* by Mötley Crüe. Is there a better song to strip to? I think not.

I have to admit, I was a bit rusty, but by the end of that first chorus, it was as if I'd never left that darkened bar with its shiny brass pole and dirty old men that were, in many cases, old enough to be my dad. Take that Jennifer Anniston! Let me show you how it's done.

As the song faded and I came to a stop, Cody was staring at me in a way that suddenly made me want to find all my clothing. Also, the little aardvark had stuck its nose out to see what was going on, if you get my meaning.

"One more?" he almost sounded like he was ready to cry. Something was wrong here.

"Deal is a deal," I scooped up my clothing and began to get dressed.

"I ain't seen a living person for weeks…since that guy convinced me to come here."

So Cody was a prisoner as well? This was getting curiouser and curiouser.

"I will make you a deal," I said as I shifted the twins around to get them in my bra just right. "You do me this little favor and I will see about getting you better living arrangements."

Of course, I had no idea how I was going to pull that off. I was simply trying to make him an offer that would get him moving towards living up to our deal.

With a sigh, Cody stood up and walked to a wall. He pushed on it and a square opened. It was like he had his own morgue. The thing was, I had not seen any indication that there were hidden drawers in the wall—and you can trust me when I say that, with my ghoulish abilities, that should not have been a problem. Not to mention that he had just produced a dead body! And now that it was here in the room, I could smell that it was relatively fresh.

*Maybe your powers are on the blink*, Mystify offered, obviously picking up on my inner monolog.

I didn't think it worked that way, but I certainly did not have the knowledge to know such things with any certainty. Something was very definitely wrong here. Come to think of it…it had been since I'd arrived.

I tried to make sense of it all, but that's not really my strong suit. I am more of a play-it-as-it-comes kind of ghoul. My best move in chess is to knock the board over if that tells you anything.

Cody had carried the body to a small dais and laid her down. He went to the bed and knelt beside it. A second later, he produced a large Hefty bag…the kind that is a dark green with a cinch at the top. He opened it and took out a handful of light brown herbs that looked like it had been left too long in one of those Ron Popeil food dehydraters.

*Incense?* I asked Adrianna.

*Hardly*, the woman snorted.

Then Cody produced a small container of rolling papers and I had my answer. I watched as the young man expertly rolled a joint and tucked it in to the corner of his mouth. Apparently satisfied, he knelt back down and produced a silver briefcase.

Within moments, he had rummaged through and found a

half dozen baggies that he carried over with him to the dais where the body had been laid out with its arms folded across its chest. He started singing something in what I was going to guess was Latin.

*Actually…* Adrianna piped up, the interest in her voice apparent, *it is a form of Sumerian that has been extinct for thousands of years.*

Meanwhile, Cody had begun to rub a few of the items from the baggies between his fingers and then on the body like he was writing something.

*Get closer*, Adrianna urged.

I moved up to the other side of the body. The smell was driving me crazy. It was so absolutely yummy…and only getting more so by the second.

*Would you think with something besides your stomach*, Adrianna scolded.

I ignored the comment as a line of drool escaped the corner of my mouth. *Damn*, I cursed, *Sharkmouth again?* There was something fundamentally wrong here. I had gotten a grip on my abilities for the most part, yet I was about as out of control as I'd been those first days; and this issue had begun just since I'd been here by my best recollection.

At last, Cody stepped back. A second or two later, the eyes on the body opened. Sure enough, he'd just created a zombie right before my eyes!

*That was odd*, Adrianna's voice in my head snapped me back to awareness.

I was about to ask what she meant when Cody blurted, "So if I make another…will you strip again?"

"No," I said with a dismissive wave. "There will be no more of that. But how many of these have you made, if you don't mind my asking?"

When he didn't say anything, I looked up to see him do that whole lock-and key thing over his lips. Really?

"Listen, you don't want to see me strip…I'm old enough to be your…" I paused, "…older aunt," I finally finished. "However, I think I can give you a better deal than to shove you down in an underground detention wing. If you escape with me, I'll bring you home and, if nothing else, you would be right across the river from Washington State where you can legally enjoy your pot."

"Yeah, but then I'd probably have to get a job."

I was struck with an idea. Admittedly it wasn't the best, but it was not horrible. "How about if I hire you to be my private chef?"

"I don't know much about cooking," Cody said skeptically.

"Maybe not for normal people." I'd endured it as long as I could. I did what ghouls do best…and a moment later, the most recently created zombie was no more.

I looked over at Cody and was suddenly as self-conscious as a porn star in church. He was looking at me with absolute horror. I guess I had just assumed that he would take it all in stride like he seemed to be doing with everything else.

"What the heck are you?" he almost cried.

"I'm a ghoul," I said. He took a few steps back; obviously that answer had not helped matters. "Listen, there is a lot that you just don't know, and I seriously don't have the time to give you the details. In short, I'm a ghoul, but, and hopefully this helps, I only eat the dead."

"You're a monster!" He was almost hysterical now. Had he not been paying attention? He was in a room full of zombies.

*But he calls them Fembots*, Adrianna said.

*Yeah? Well I can call my breasts perky…that does not necessarily make them so*, I snapped.

*No, but I don't think he has any idea what he is doing.*

I tried a new tactic. "Who taught you how to make zom—" I snapped my mouth shut and took a quick breath. "Fembots. Who taught you how to make Fembots?"

"My Uncle Perry."

"And where is he now?" I asked.

"He died a few years ago."

"I'm sorry."

"Don't be…he was a dick."

I didn't have time to hear his family woes. I pointed to the zombie that was in the worst shape of the bunch. Her skin was a sickly greenish blue and bits of her face had sloughed off leaving more exposed skull than anything else. "And why do you think she is coming apart like that?"

"Batteries. But I don't know how to recharge them. Uncle Perry never showed me that bit." And then, almost inaudible to the point that I almost missed it, "His never fell apart…wonder how he did it?"

"What?" In my head I heard Adrianna ask the same question. I thought that I detected what might be a bit of jealousy.

Cody looked up at me and blinked his large, brown, blood-shot eyes. I'd already determined that he was a young, twenty-something, but at that very moment, he looked like a little boy who was lost, confused, and frightened.

"My uncle had a dozen Fembots out at his farm, they never seemed to sleep…and they sure didn't fall apart. It's just like he always said…I'm a screw up. Just like my dad."

Again, as sad as it was, I just didn't have the time for his therapy. He was saying something that, judging by Adrianna's palpable agitation, was of great importance.

"Think, Cody," I urged. "Was there anything that you saw your uncle do with the…Fembots? Anything different or strange?"

Cody looked like he was constipated more than anything else as he thought. He squeezed his eyes shut and scrunched up his face. After several seconds I was ready to give up hope. After all, I was asking a Generation-Y stereotype to focus on something that was not a video game or marijuana.

An idea came. I have no idea where from; I had just finished reading a book series that Lisa discovered a while back. It was something about white trash zombies or some such nonsense. She had said that there was far too much realism in the pages for this to simply be somebody's imagination. If I was right, I was going to have to go back and read that book series again…well, I could think about that later.

"Brains!" I blurted.

*You can't be serious*, Adrianna scoffed.

*I am absolutely serious*, I shot back at her.

*Fiction...absolute fiction*, Mystify snorted.

*Yeah? Well that is what the general public thinks when it comes to a lot of their favorite book series. We know better though, don't we?* I snapped.

Now I only had one problem: where was I going to find some brains? I felt more than heard Adrianna titter at that thought.

I was going to have to do something bad. But if this was for the greater good, then wasn't it worth it? My inner argument was a heated one. To explore this option, I would have to kill somebody or something. I was determined to have this issue solved before the sun set. For some reason, it was important to me that I deal with this before Claude or any of his upstairs minions came down here. I wanted to have a little something in place to deal with that scoundrel.

"Just stay put," I said to Cody.

"Where are you going?" he whined. "You aren't leaving are you?"

"Not any further than just down the hallway."

"Promise?"

Okay, can I just say that I have some real problems with the so-called "sensitive male"? I'm not saying that guys are not allowed to have feelings, but there is a point where it just gets to be too much. There is a difference between showing emotions and just being a big pussy. Seriously, there really is no nice way to say that.

"Yeah," I said with a nod, but I was already headed out the door. I did not like what I was about to do.

Next, on a Very Special *That Ghoul Ava...*

## 5

# Some Heads Are Gonna Roll

I looked at the cavernous hallway with its doors all along the length. I was trying to recall what sorts of heads had peered out from which ones.

*Think about this, Ava,* Adrianna was lecturing. *What you are about to do is based on a guess from a book that, as I recall, was very pedestrian. Seriously, how can you take any stock in something so flimsy?*

I went through the process of locking her away. Interestingly enough, Mystify had gone silent. Perhaps he was curious and, after seeing how I'd just dealt with his…roommate? Brainmate? Hmm… Anyways, maybe he just did not want to be locked away.

I stopped at a door. Damn! My super senses were not giving me any help here. I was not hearing a thing. That had me concerned. It felt like I had been out of whack ever since arriving here. Something was definitely wrong, but I would have to take things one problem at a time.

Bracing myself for what was to come, I opened the door. My first thought was relief that I had guessed correctly.

"Come for a little something special, ghoul," the goblin snarled. He reached down and clutched at his obscenely disproportionate genitals and waggled them in my direction. The bastard had the gall to wink! Maybe this would be easier than I thought.

I closed the door behind me and willed my fingers and toes into their deadly versions. To his credit, the goblin's face did not change much.

"Ahh…a bit of what the humans call foreplay." He sprang up onto a table and had a blade in his hand. I could not even begin to fathom where he'd kept it hidden. "Well then, perhaps I will make you the bloody bitch of my harem when this is over. I like a bit of sport before sticking it in."

I swear, goblins are just the nastiest creatures. I was going to have a chat with Nose Wart when I returned home. He had seemed just as vile when we first met, but now…well…he was more like a puppy…a very flatulent puppy, but still, that comparison works.

"I am sorry for what I have to do," I said as I moved his direction.

"The only thing you will have to do is service me," the goblin roared.

With that, he launched himself. Honestly, it caught me by surprise, and I barely managed to swat away his blade with my claws. I was still not quite up to speed on the whole fighting thing, and found myself backing up as the tiny creature that barely came to my mid-thigh turned into a whirling dervish.

After what seemed like forever, he came to a stop. Flecks of spittle came from his mouth and nose as he panted heavily. I had not scored so much as a nick, but I could feel a couple of stinging spots where he had slashed me.

"Tired yet?" he managed between gasps for air.

I had to give the little guy credit, he was no quitter. Admittedly, I was a bit tired as well from swatting all—or at least most—of his slashes away with my claws. *It is time to end his suffering.* I'm not entirely sure where that thought came from, but I agreed with the sentiment.

I took a step forward, and the goblin brought his blade up in anticipation of my attack. I could see his arms trembling from fatigue. A very distant voice in my head screamed for me to rethink things. There had to be a better way…or at least a way that did not involve my having to commit murder. Unfortunately, that voice was drowned out by a new sound.

A roar? I had no idea where it came from at first. Actually, I thought it was the goblin, but his lips were pressed together tighter than a straight man's butt cheeks at a Village People concert.

*That's you, you idiot*, Mystify's voice echoed from a dark corridor of my mind.

I brought my claws down in a flash and shattered the goblin's sword like it was made from spun sugar instead of metal. All ten switch-digits found a home in the tiny thing's flesh; and just as quickly, exited from the opposite side. I'd basically turned him in to the equivalent of a stack of goblin bologna…or baloney; I never know which is right, or if there is even a difference. His head rolled a few feet and stopped.

And just like that, I was a killer.

Now, to be fair, I'd killed before. The very first time had been the bastard that had gotten Lisa pregnant; but I hardly classified that individual as human. Also, I'd met more decent monsters…so there is that. No, this was the killing of a living creature to serve my own needs. I had done this just so that I could test a theory.

All of a sudden, I wondered how scientists in research facilities did not all just end their days slitting their wrists. You can make any excuse that you want, but if you are dumping mascara into the eyes of little bunny rabbits or infecting monkeys with a variety of diseases just so that you can test an experimental medicine on them and don't feel like the lowest form of pond scum, then you probably have no soul and are not even deserving of my pity.

I picked up the head and just as quickly dropped it when the eyes blinked at me. I moved around to be sure that the eyes did not follow me. Once I was certain that they weren't, and I was able to chalk that up to some sort of post-death involuntary reflex, I was able to pick the head up once more and exit the room.

I was standing in the hallway when a couple of the doors

opened. I saw Theodore the Owlbear and a few others peering at me. Huh, what do you know...an owl's eyes can get wider.

I certainly was not doing myself any favors standing here with a goblin head in my hand. These folks were already treating me like *I* was a monster. Oh...wait...I am, but you know what I mean. After all, I'm still Ava Birch; just a normal gal from Portland, Oregon who happens to also be a ghoul.

"Everybody back in your rooms, there is nothing to see here," I yelled.

The chorus of doors slamming was almost comical...only, one of the doors didn't shut, it flew open. Out stepped (you probably guessed it) a female goblin. She had her hands on her hips and was giving me a look that should have been able to inflict physical harm. I'd never been looked at with such hatred. Honestly, I did not care for it in the slightest.

"What have you done?" the female goblin demanded with a curling of her lips that revealed some impressive teeth.

"I am really sorry, and I would like to talk about this, but now is kind of a bad time," I answered weakly. Something in me was fighting to break loose. I could feel it, and it was very unpleasant.

Have you ever heard some story or another about a crazy psycho killer who gets caught and says that he claims that he heard voices in his head (yeah, I said he, not many female, crazed psycho killers out there last I checked)? Well, there was something like that brewing in my own head that had nothing to do with the additional occupants currently taking up residence in there. It was dark and mean and nasty. Something told me that it was very important to keep whatever *that* was sealed away for as long as possible.

"You are a ghoul!" the goblin stated, pointing out what I considered to be the obvious. "Ghouls are never sorry."

"Yeah? Well you haven't met me, but you are going to have to take my word for it."

"I challenge you!" the goblin bellowed, and came at me at an all-out sprint.

Why didn't people understand me when I said I didn't have

time for nonsense? Even worse, this female goblin was unarmed; I was going to have to take her down, and she wasn't carrying so much as a pea shooter.

About ten feet away, the little creature launched itself, claws out and teeth barred. It was not even close to fair. With a simple backhand, I took the head off. The only plus to the entire incident was that I now had two brains to use in my experiment.

I returned to Cody's room with both heads. Okay, I really had not given any thought to the situation. I should have realized that the young man was going to freak out. Oh…and he did…big time.

"What in the hell are those?" Cody was cowering on his bed.

The strange part was that he was hiding behind three female zombies. Didn't he understand the whole part about how he was using undead to shield himself from something as relatively harmless as a pair of severed goblin heads?

"Where did you think I was going to obtain brains? These are heads, you idiot," I closed the door behind me.

"I know they are heads…but *what* are they?" he repeated his question with a bit more emphasis.

*You have got to be kidding*, I thought. He has been down here for how long and he has not seen any of the other denizens of the holding cells? That was ridiculous.

"So let me get this straight," I said as I used my switchfingers to split one of the heads open. "You never leave this room? You simply stay in here…get stoned…and make zo—Fembots?" I was getting tired of sugar-coating things for this kid.

"Pretty much," Cody answered with a shrug.

"I weep for the new generation."

*Now you know how I feel*, Adrianna muttered.

I plucked the gray lump of goblin brain and held it up. Instantly, all of the zombies turned my direction. It was the first time they seemed to actually take notice of my presence. However, their dead eyes were still not really seeing me; it was clear that their focus was on what I held in my hand.

"Come get your yummy goblin brains," I sing-songed.

"Did you say goblin brains?" The skepticism in Cody's voice was thick.

"It was a risk, but goblins are probably the easiest thing to come by down here. I sure wasn't going to kill the owlbear or the mud troll."

Sure, I could have been a bit gentler with my reply, but I needed this kid to snap out of his human daze and open his eyes to the realm of the Supernaturals. Wait…did I just say that? A plan was starting to formulate, but I did not have time to babysit a mortal.

While Cody was sputtering nonsense about how this could not be real, I gave a lobe of brain to the first pair of zombies that reached me. They stuffed it into their mouths and I had just a second to appreciate why Lisa had never wanted to be present when I ate. However, I was able to visibly observe the deterioration actually recede as the zombies feasted.

Okay…maybe "feasted" is stretching it a bit. They each only got about two or three bites. What happened could have almost been considered funny if I'd had the time to appreciate it; the zombies started pawing at me, tugging on my pockets and sniffing at me like a puppy would if he thought that his or her master had treats hidden somewhere on their person.

*How can this be?* Adrianna was obviously upset by this revelation. My response was how could she have overlooked something so simple? Seriously, just say the word "zombie" to a group of people and somebody will moan the word "braa-a-a-iins" within seconds. Go ahead and try it…see if I'm wrong.

"Okay, so we know that bit…all we need to do now is figure out a way—"

Cody's scream cut me off. I turned to see all of the recently fed zombies pawing at him. If I didn't know any better, I would say—

And then he screamed again. This time it was much different. This was a scream of pain. His own zombies were eating him.

*How can that be?* Adrianna voiced yet another question of which I had no answer.

I bounded across the room and did the only thing that I could think of. I'm not proud of it. I mean, I would like to say that I was able to exert some form of control, but the moment I gave myself permission to feed…it was a frenzy.

When it was all said and done, all of the zombies were gone. And, as for Cody…well…he was sort of dessert. When I came back in control of myself, I saw his eyes roll back in his head. At first I just thought he had passed out. There was a lot of blood on the sheets. And then the smell hit me. I knew before his eyes opened what I would see.

*This is all wrong*, Adrianna insisted. *Zombies should not do that. They don't feed on their master…ever. And the condition does not spread via the bite.*

*Well I think you need to amend that statement*, I replied right before I sent Cody down my gullet to join his Fembots.

*Not just that*, Adrianna continued, *but this is just…wrong.*

I could sense her frustration, but at the moment, I had bigger fish to fry. We were still being held prisoner in the basement of a Psychic who I was pretty sure might be suffering from *Pinky and the Brain* syndrome. Basically, I think he was trying to take over the world. At least the Supernatural part of it anyway.

*And what do you think you can do to stop him?* Adrianna asked. Now, it could have been a snarky and sarcastic comment; but actually, it sounded like she was genuinely interested.

"I guess I will have to kill him."

*Whoa…where the hell am I?* a familiar voice slurred from somewhere in my head.

"Crap," I mumbled, but very similar sentiments were echoed by Mystify and Adrianna.

Next, on a Very Special *That Ghoul Ava...*

# 6

## Turn Me Loose

"Oh, miss, I don't know if I can do that," Gretch was practically crying. I had her all upset, but I knew that we did not have a lot of time to make some sort of elaborate plan.

After leaving Cody's room and sealing him away in my mind where I could deal with him later, I had gone up and down the length of the corridor and peeked in on every resident—such as it was. When I was done—and besides Gretch—I had counted forty-seven goblins, nineteen bugbears, Theodore the Owlbear, and two gnomes. Funny…they looked exactly like the little garden statues that are so popular.

"We don't really have a choice. I have a feeling that Claude is up to no good."

*You can say that again*, Mystify grumbled. For some reason, he was either really good at slipping my containment, or else I was just forgetting to lock him up.

"But you are asking me…us," Gretch waved her hands at the door where a few of the more eager goblins waited, "to do something that violates all our laws."

It is no surprise that the goblins were immediately up for this plan. Of course, I'm quickly learning that, if there is a chance for a fight, you don't even have to ask when it comes to goblin participation. It is what the little monsters live for from what little I have learned about them up to this point.

"I am asking for you to avenge your former Psychic," I repeated for what I had to guess must be the tenth time.

It is odd, but the one creature that I thought might be the most supportive of dishing out a little "get back" on this usurping Psychic was the biggest heel-digger of the bunch. In fact, I'd been counting on her support to win over the equally reluctant Theodore the Owlbear.

"You are asking us to violate the laws under which we have always lived," Gretch insisted.

Honestly, when you are trying to argue your point, saying the exact same thing over and over does not really cut it. It is like that Monty Python routine about paying for an argument. John Cleese keeps simply saying "No you didn't" to the adorable Michael Palin. So far, Gretch had been using practically the same method in her refusal to take part in my plan. Sure, it was a flimsy one, but the goblins seemed to like it. My plan, that is.

"What I am asking you to do is stand up for yourselves. You had a Psychic who tended to your needs and did all the stuff Psychics do..." Although, honestly, I really still have no idea what that is. "All I am asking is for you to step up and help me put this guy in his place. He has no right to keep you all locked up down here."

Of course, if I was being completely honest, he had made his biggest mistake in locking *me* up down here. Nobody puts baby in the corner...or in a sunshine protected basement jail.

So I bet you are probably wondering just what it is that I have planned. Well, here is how I put it to the goblins once I got them to stop grabbing their junk and making lewd comments.

"The sun is going to set soon. From what I have seen, this Claude has a few vampires and revenants that serve him. He obviously is relying on your observance of protocol to keep you in line. Add to that the fact that he has a mansion that is almost the proverbial glass house..."

Did I forget to mention that part when I first got here? Yeah, when I arrived by taxi, I had to admit that I was totally blown away by the amount of windows. Considering the fact that Psychics are part of the Supernatural community, I was sort of confused. I asked Mystify what the deal was with all the windows and he said that it was actually just a form of protection. When I asked from what, he said that not all districts were like Portland. Apparently, the Supernatural community is always just on the edge of open conflict. Centuries of being shoved into the dark has allowed for some serious resentment to build. And get this, some of the Supernaturals are actually hoping for this war with the Templars!

"The Psychic that many of you knew has been replaced by this Claude person. Now, I realize that none of you goblins or any of you who might be related to the faeries have any committed tie to the regional Psychic, but I can also bet that none of you are ready to have Templars roll in and start crossing you off of their to-do list."

"We fear no...Templar!" one of the goblins had snorted in that strange way they have of speaking like they don't really know what they are saying so much as mimicking sounds that they have heard before.

"Then stay here and live in this basement for all I care. I could give a vampire's bloody discharge what you fear or don't fear. Hide down in this jail and die like mangy dogs," I said with a shrug...and then I spat on the floor.

Yeah, I know...that was kind of gross, but when talking to goblins, I have learned in my brief exposure that you don't talk to them like you would anything else. And they are not only big on curses and what we might consider cut downs, but they always spit.

That had gotten them all to gather around a few of the ones that I would suspect had to be the leaders. Unfortunately, all goblins look alike to me, so I would be hard pressed to pick out the ones that seemed to be left with the decision.

Of course, the entire time, Gretch was almost a blubbering mess. And that, in turn, had Mystify upset. If I didn't know better, I would think that he and that mud troll were doing the nasty. And I am not saying that in a manner of slang. Seriously, if he was doing Gretch...it was nasty.

Theodore the Owlbear actually became enthusiastic the more I spoke. He kept fluffing those feathers around his head and making this hoot that would end in a bit of a growl. I didn't have the heart to tell him that it was absolutely adorable.

That is probably not what a male of any sort wants to hear when they are acting tough. But seriously, it sort of reminded me of The New Kids on the Block. They had a song called "Hanging Tough" that got fairly popular. They were just the cutest little guys in that video. Who knew that little Donnie Wahlberg would grow up to be such a bad ass? Still, when you are fourteen or fifteen…

Anyways, back to my plan; the bugbears were the easiest sell. They wanted out of this basement in the worst way.

"We smash and kill?" one of the huge beasts grumbled.

"And eat if you want," I added.

That was all that it had taken to sway them. All I had left were the gnomes. I was considering just leaving them out of it. I mean, they are *gnomes*!

"Pardon the boldness of my interruption, Madame Ghoul," a very proper English-accented voice spoke.

Imagine my surprise when I discovered that the two gnomes had climbed up on my shoulder. They smelled earthy and like a grassy field right after it rains. It was strange, but they did not smell like…food. This must be more of that internal protection stuff that Morgan had talked about.

"Umm…" Okay, I had nothing. I mean…you try to say something when the mascot for Travelocity is standing on your shoulder. Oh yeah, and how he and his cohort got there is still a mystery to me.

"We would be quite honored if you would allow us the pleasure to join in your assault on the upper bastion." This came from the gnome on my other shoulder. It was sort of like those cartoons where there is an angel on one side and a devil on the other…except they were both gnomes.

"The…bastion?" *Damn, I bet that word is in my calendar.*

*He means the house*, Mystify prompted.

"If you would allow it, Madame Ghoul, we could slip out

first and perhaps make a go of finding the Psychic." It was like a tennis match in slow motion. Then it struck me as to what this pair reminded me of now that I'd had a moment. The Goofy Gophers from the old Warner Brothers cartoons. Go ahead and set this book down for a moment and Google it; I'll wait.

Yeah…those two.

I wasn't going to turn down help…no matter how small. One of my problems as a newbie to the Supernatural community is the fact that I think too much like a human. I have been told that a hundred times or more. Perhaps these little fellas have some sort of super powers. I got no idea.

Once it was agreed, all I had left to convince was Gretch. Through this entire ordeal, she had been a blubbering mess. Oh, and when a mud troll cries, they leak actual mud. I decided to take a risk. I grabbed her by the arm and led her to her room while everybody else went and did whatever it is that they felt they needed to do before this possible battle. For the goblins, it apparently meant sex. Yep, right there in the hall. On the floors, up against the walls…didn't matter. Oh yeah, Nose Wart and I were going to have a nice long sit down when I got home.

Once Gretch and I were in her room, I shut the door. "Okay, I need you to listen. Also…I *really* need you to keep a secret. Can you do that?"

The pathetic creature nodded. She gave a horrid sniff and I could actually see the twin trails of troll snot get sucked back up each nostril. I was doing okay until she made an exaggerated swallow. I gave an involuntary shudder and sat down beside the little thing.

"Mystify is here."

I let that sort of hang for a moment.

*Umm…perhaps you should rethink this.* Damn…how did Adrianna get out?

"I know what I am doing," I said out loud.

"I would never presume to question," Gretch mumbled in her gurgling voice that was made worse by the crying.

*Trolls of this sort are not difficult to break*, Adrianna insisted.

59

*As much as it pains me, I have to agree*, Mystify added. *Duuude!*

Great! All three of them were out. I really needed to get a handle on this containment thing.

"Gretch, I need you to trust me on this. Claude has something going on here, and he sent Mystify into another Psychic's territory with the knowledge that it would not go well. As it would happen…I ate him."

The wail that came from the mud troll was enough to hurt my ears. It was this high-pitched noise like the kind that would shatter a crystal wine glass.

"I didn't know what was happening," I said in a weak defense.

*And you do now?* Adrianna quipped.

*I am so going to eat you a second time as soon as I figure out how*, I snarled, making extra sure that I kept that comment inside.

"He showed up…and then he started coming at me with all these lies."

*You have no idea what is going around you, Ava.* Mystify sounded almost apologetic. *There is a war coming, and you are in the center of it.*

That was new. Not the war part. I'd been hearing that a lot lately. The new part was the thing about me being in the center of it. I had a lot of homework to do when I got out of this damn Supernatural holding center.

My eyes went back to Gretch. She was actually starting to melt into a slurry of brown goo. I needed to get my head locked on. Something about this little troll had gotten to me. She was like one of those puppies from the Sarah McLachlan commercials.

"You have to trust me, Gretch," I said in as soothing a voice as I could manage. Truthfully, I was getting a little annoyed. She was behaving like one of those women who got slapped and then acted as if they deserved it. I hated women like that…nobody deserves to be abused.

"But there is an order to things," she insisted.

"Okay…and where do you fall in that order?"

"I am a mud troll, I would think that said all there was to be said."

"Enlighten me…share some of this order crap with an ignorant ghoul."

"Besides the fact that trolls are unwelcome hybrids, I am a mud troll. That puts me at the lowest of all my kin," Gretch sniffed.

"Who makes this stuff up?" I demanded. I let that question rattle around inside my head as well as outside.

*I was unaware, I can offer you no help here*, Adrianna finally replied.

Mystify was strangely silent. Perhaps it was too painful for him to see a creature that he obviously had such strong feelings in such obvious personal torment.

"It is what I was told…taught from early on." Gretch looked up at me. Her saucer eyes were leaking brown drizzles that ran in rivulets down her ruddy face.

"Okay, and where do ghouls fall in this order?" I asked. Part of it was out of genuine curiosity, but since I had an angle and an idea of the answers I was about to receive, I awaited her predictable reply.

"Ghouls are not in the order."

Umm…okay. That was absolutely *not* the answer that I had expected.

"What do you mean?" I had just shot way past curious.

"Ghouls answer to no being. They are rumored to be the most fierce warriors, and void of any emotion or feeling."

*A*-ha! I shouted that bit inside my head. Judging by the grumbles from Adrianna and even Cody, I did so at a rather excessive volume. "So do you think I am void of any emotion or feeling?"

Now I may have a few exes out there who have a less-than-flattering response to that query, but I doubted that I came across that way to most people who lack an personal attachment in response to that question. I looked Gretch in the eyes and tried to force something that might convey emotion into my own. The only problem was that they were a pair of solid black orbs and I had no idea what anybody or anything might see in them, if they bothered to look.

"N-n-no," came the reply in a barely audible whisper.

"But you said..." I tried to make that statement end on a high note that I sort of sing-songed; almost like I might be teasing playfully.

"I just don't—" she started, but an eruption of noise form the hallway cut her off.

I jumped to my feet and ran to the door, throwing it open. The headless body of a revenant flew past and landed with an ugly squishing sound on the stone floor.

"Ava Birch!" a man's voice yelled with some pretty apparent anger. To put not too fine of a point on it...Claude was pissed.

# 7

# Venus

"Claude...darling," I cooed as I came out into the hall.

Four bugbears each had a grip on a limb belonging to a revenant. Sadly, for the rev at least, those limbs were no longer attached to the flopping, blood-squirting torso that was kind of writhing on the floor. There was a dogpile of goblins and I could only suppose that another revenant was at the bottom.

As for Claude, he was in an owlbear hug just inside the door. No wonder he sounded so cranky. Theodore was a bonafide cutie, but he smelled like...well...an owlbear, and he had quite a grip if Claude's facial hue of beet red was any indication.

"I...demand...to...be...put...down," Claude gasped between each breath. Which, from the sound of his weakening voice, was becoming more and more difficult to suck in after each exhale.

"You demand?" Now it was my turn to sound like a Bond villain. "Claude, my sweet, you are in no position to make any demands."

His eyes bulged as Theodore grunted and gave just a bit tighter of a squeeze. Much more, and he was going to absorb the Psychic into his fur and feathers.

"You are making a mistake." If not for my exceptional ghoul hearing, which had suddenly come back in spades, I might not have actually been able to hear those words.

"You know," I walked up and placed a hand on Theodore's shoulder, "I hear that a lot. The funny thing is that how, much like when a parent feels the need to constantly scream at his or her kids, you learn to tune it out after a while. Morgan has been singing me that little ditty for quite a while, so you need to come up with something that will penetrate the barriers I seem to have erected."

"You are in danger...the Templars are coming for you."

*Okay, that would do it*, I thought with a grimace.

"Theodore, drop him."

The owlbear took me at my literal best. Claude landed on the cold, hard stone with a meaty thump. I was not about to give back this little advantage and sprang into action. Pouncing on the downed Psychic, I willed my switchfingers into being and put one sharp, pointy index blade right under his chin. I was not entirely sure that Claude was not immune or immortal or whatever, but I was betting that he could not ignore pain like a ghoul.

"Start talking, Sparky," I hissed, my lips just a hair's breadth from his as I brought on Sharkmouth.

He looked up at me, and I thought that there was a trace of fear in those dreamy eyes.

"Misssss Birch," a familiar voice hissed.

I felt my blood run cold. Okay, I know that is a used up saying, and my blood is already room temperature, but that did not lessen the degree that I felt all oogie inside.

A while back, I was snatched from my home and taken to a place near Albany. I knew that it was Albany just because of the smell. No offense if you are from Albany, Oregon...but your town can get pretty stinky. I'm not exactly saying something you don't know. Anyways, I was taken to some dark room and a bunch of goblins did some pretty nasty things to me including a double mastectomy. Lucky me...ghouls have regenerative powers.

While I was held, a voice spoke with me, made a bunch of promises, and then took me home. I had some time to think and I believed that whoever or—more likely—*whatever* this mystery voice was, they sent me home so that I would do bad things. When a ghoul has been seriously injured, they must feed to recover. They enter a state called *Fame Rabia*. That is Latin for "really hungry" or something. What it boiled down to was that I was like a shark in a feeding frenzy; I didn't care who or what I ate.

So, you probably guessed...the owner of the mystery voice was here. Only, this time, I was not helpless, and there were not a bunch of goblins ripping me apart. In fact, I had my own little army of beasties ready to do some damage. In fact, my minions were charging the stairs and the dark figure standing in the doorway.

"Everybody freeze!" I barked.

I would probably hate myself for this. You never let up on the evil villain once you have them in your sights. They always get away, do more damage—usually worse than anything that they have done in the past—and then there is a second confrontation where the hero wins and saves the day. Funny how nobody gives that hero a swift kick in the ass for not ending the bad guy the first time they had the chance.

My goblins were not all that interested in following orders that did not involve killing. A dozen of them were halfway up the stairs when a blue flash flickered from the as yet still unidentified dark figure. Just that fast, they were goblin-pops...goblin-cicles...basically frozen solid is what I am getting at.

There was a brief second or two of silence; and then the frozen goblins toppled and shattered like very fragile glass. The smell hit me and I almost lost it. Basically, if Ben & Jerry's had a smell...this was the ghoul equivalent. I shoved my hunger down and took a step forward.

"How about you come out so that we can meet more formally?" I said, gripping one of the bugbears by its big, hairy arm and pulling it back behind me. Yay me for keeping my cool!

I heard an honest-to-goodness cackle like some sort of Wicked Witch of the West wanna-be, then the dark shape took a step forward and into the flickering light of the corridor.

At first I almost laughed, but then I quickly recalled that

thinking like a human can get me into big trouble. This frail, stooped over, wart-faced, long nosed old hag wearing what looked like a ratty, ash-colored gunny sack turned into a dress stepped into view. The hair was wispy and almost white, at least what I could see of it. She was wearing this funny shaped hat that looked like a lopsided square version of the classic witch cone-shaped hat. Her eyes were the only thing about her that stood out as remarkable in their beauty. They were sapphire blue and sparkled with obvious Supernatural light. I actually expected to see little beams like those from a flashlight coming from them they were so dazzling. The two legs that jutted out from the bottom of the gunny sack were spindly and had coarse black hairs. Somebody needed to order herself an Epilady. Personally, I believe shaving is something that we women are trained to do in order to stop men from petting us. Our body hair distracts them too much or something.

All I could think was that it was like the first time that I had met one of my favorite radio DJs. He had this voice that made me all tingly. He looked like he had never met a doughnut that he didn't like, and his thinning hair was a greasy mess and in serious need of shampoo *and* conditioner. To put it plainly, the voice did not match what I was seeing in my mind.

When it came to my latest villain, I could not have been more wrong or off the mark. For one, I had honestly thought that this was a dude. And then there was the whole comparing it to an alien spider. I certainly was not expecting—

"Blodwen Cadwallader, Queen of the Celtic Mulingar Gwyllion, Holder of the Blue Sphere, Cosantóir of the Ten Sidhe, but my friends call me Muffy."

Okay, now I could not help it. I know it probably cost me points with my minions, but I started laughing. It was a snicker at first, but then it just turned into something that I could not control. Pretty soon I was leaning against a bugbear so I didn't fall on my butt.

"M-m-muffy?" I sputtered, still chuckling like a loon. "I think I am gonna go with Blodwen."

"Actually," the hag took another step, "you will address me

as Queen Cadwallader."

Blodwen stepped down one of the stone stairs that put her in the midst of the shattered remnants of the goblins that she had turned to ice. The torches on the wall flared and seemed to suddenly brighten the corridor considerably. I noticed a few of the bugbears actually shield their eyes, and Theodore the Owlbear scuttled behind as if seeking me for protection; unfortunately for Claude, Theodore had not loosed his grip and dragged the Psychic most unceremoniously.

I was about to make a snarky comment when the bitch changed. In a single step, she did that crazy morphing thing. Suddenly she was almost six feet tall. Her body was slender in that very unfair way. You know how some girls get stupid and think that skinny to the point of being able to see each rib is sexy? Not this gal, old Blodwen was now like the freaking human equivalent of the Venus de Milo. And that ash gunny sack? It had turned into this clingy, form fitting gown that looked like it had been spun from liquid silver. Her hair framed a sickeningly pretty face…but the eyes, they were still freakishly blue in a very unnatural way.

"I think it is time we talk," Blodwen said in a voice that now matched her body, face, and…well…everything. Basically, she sounded like just the sweetest thing. Imagine a real estate agent who only shows million dollar homes.

*Tread with caution, Ava.* Mystify was suddenly right back in the mix. *This one is a fey of incredible power.*

"Grrgl," a strangled voice wheezed from behind me.

"Theodore, I think that you can set Claude down." I risked a quick glance over my shoulder. Blodwen did not strike me as the sort to make a sneak attack. This one wanted you to know what was coming, because there was probably nothing that you could do to stop it. "But," I held up one cautionary finger, "if he so much as twitches…rip his head off and give it to the goblins for a soccer ball."

"What is soccer balls?" I heard one of the goblins mutter. There was a meaty smack and a yelp.

"I just sockered your balls!" another goblin brayed with a

laugh that only sounded odd because it was coming from a goblin— at least I think it was a different goblin.

"So, what do you reckon we have to discuss?" I asked.

"For one..." Blodwen took another step closer, her eyes locked on me, "when we met, I told you to let things be with the faeries. I said that it was handled. I gave you explicit instructions to butt out and tell Morgan-the-Meddler to do so as well."

"I hate to be the one to break this to you, but if I listened to what I was told...well, I just wouldn't be me," I answered truthfully. "And have you met Morgan? I don't know that anybody tells her what to do. And if you were serious about wanting to tell her something like that, I am the last one you want delivering that message. She and I don't exactly see eye-to-eye." Wow...talk about a huge understatement.

"You killed Prince Fraylee. He was the last of the oldest faerie bloodline. Do you have any idea what that means?"

"Not really."

"It puts a new house in power."

"Look," I shook my head, "I think you should just try to tell me what you want me to know. I am not all that up to date on the ins and outs of the Supernatural world. Nobody really tells me anything."

"The faerie are governed by the ruling house." Suddenly old Bloddy was a schoolmarm lecturing the class idiot. "All of faerie kind must follow the edicts set forth from the ruling house. What you saw...that silly little mall incident, that was childish mischief.

"When the Godmother was assassinated, Merriette was acting like a child who had just inherited a fortune and had no idea how to deal with it. THAT was where I was prepared to come in and settle things down."

I gave this woman an appraising look. She seemed sincere. And the funny thing was that she did not come across anything at all like the thing that had brought me in to be tortured and abused. I was missing something...as usual.

"Did you know about the prince and the little army he was creating? The mutations or whatever you want to call them that he was purposefully creating for some war that he was going to wage against the Templars? I have a trio of jötnar living with me for crying out loud!" I felt my anger start to build.

This Blodwen was either completely ignorant or did not care that an attempt had been made to revive an ancient war. To make matters worse, it was being staged to look as if the Supernatural community was in on it. I had averted it, thank you very much.

"If my reports are correct," Blodwen countered, "they were only interested in eliminating those deemed unholy…the undead such as vampires—"

"And ghouls!" I snarled.

Before I knew it, my switchfingers came on. I liked the fact that I could bring them on when I wanted, but I hated when they simply popped out of their own accord. I wonder if this is how men feel about their little soldier. Many a teen male has been embarrassed by the inadvertent woody during gym class.

Blodwen leaped back, and just that quick, she was the old crone version once more. That had me wondering which form of her was the real one. Maybe later I could ponder on it, but at the moment I had a head of righteous steam building…and apparently a bit of an advantage. I may not know much, but I know a look of fear when I see it.

"I got the full measure of their hate for all things that *they* deemed unholy," I pressed my point. "But I can say with as much certainty as possible that I am far from unholy. I am not bothered the slightest by crosses, holy water, or anything else that has to do with religion."

"That proves nothing!" the detached spider-like voice was back. I was now certain that I did not like this version of old Bloddy. "You are no longer in possession of your soul. You are an abomination!"

Whoa! Wait…what?

"What do you mean by that whole me not having my soul thing?"

Nobody had told me anything like that. Why is it that every single time I start to make some ground in getting a grasp on this Supernatural thing, somebody tosses me another nasty curve that sends me spiraling out of control like Sandra Bullock in that movie *Gravity*?

"You took your life...did you not?" Blodwen asked with no emotion.

"Umm...yeah..." A torrent of bad memories came flooding in with a fury that almost buckled my knees.

I had reached a part of my life where I had simply given up. It is strange, but I am happier now as a ghoul than I ever was a living person. I feel like I have a purpose. Sure, I was always screwing something up, and I had a hard time divorcing myself from thinking like a human, but I felt like I had place in the world. Heck, I had just diverted a possible Supernatural extinction event.

"You had your chance and chose to squander a gift so precious," Blodwen said with a finger pointed in accusation.

"Okay, first...you don't know anything about me. And while I am certainly not the best person to call on for a morality spokesman, what makes you the ethical center of the universe? I know ghosts...well, just one, but she is a peach. And vampires, while I am not a fan, there are some that, much like humans, are better than others. The moment that you start painting everybody with the same brush, you cover up a lot of good things."

Wow...I had no idea I had that sort of thing inside me. I was never going to be called upon to be a keynote speaker or the leader of some activist group. Still, you can't put everybody into the same box.

I'd already learned so much in these past few months. I even had a goblin that I was not completely repulsed by. If I was being honest with myself, I was starting to really warm to Nose Wart.

And then something else hit me. It was the follow up punch, and this one hurt bad.

# It's the End of the World as We Know It (And I Feel Fine)

"Lisa…I am so sorry," I whispered.

When I got home, I would seek her out and beg for her to forgive my being such an idiot. How many times did she have to tell me that she had my back no matter what? Just because she was training to become a Templar did not mean that she had stopped being Lisa. I had lumped her in with a group that I really did not know much about besides the stories and the secondhand information that I'd let *others* feed me.

Then my head popped up and I took a look around this dank dungeon-esque corridor.

"Pardon?" Blodwen tilted her head. Her eyes remained fixed on my fingers and I retracted them. Just that fast, she morphed back to the pretty version. I would have to test that later. Right now, I had bigger things to worry about. Something had brought at least two of us here under what I was starting to think might be false pretense. I glanced at Claude…where did he fit? Was he masterminding some sort of elaborate plan?

I shook my head to clear it. This was wrong…all wrong. As usual, I could not put a finger on it, but there was a huge piece of the puzzle that I was missing.

It had begun long before my "chance" meeting with Mystify. Just as in the world of humans, there were a select few in the upper echelon that were trying to steer all of the supposed lesser beings on the course that they chose.

"Why are you here?" I asked Blodwen. "What would bring you all the way to Texas and the home of a Psychic who has somehow managed to send his predecessor to the territory of another? You were the one who went to great lengths to warn me to stay out of the faerie business. And you extended that warning to Morgan. Yet…here you are in the house of another Psychic. One who may or may not be a shady bastard."

"Wait…who told you that I had anything to do with sending Mystify to Portland?" Claude asked indignantly.

I spun on the man and felt a part of me turn to water. I know that I am totally hooked on Brett Michaels, but Vince Neal was absolutely dee-lish! Claude looked like he stepped right out of the "Dr. Feelgood" video. His long hair was that perfect peroxide blond, and he even wore a purple headband with some sort of weird slitted eye stitched in hot pink. It was like an eye, but the pupil was wrong…shaped funny. He was decked out in some tight leather pants and a flowing purple top that looked like it was made from silk.

*Beware, Ava*, Mystify chimed in my head.

*Hey…who is that guy?* I heard Cody pipe up.

Then there was, and bear with my attempt to describe it, the sound of a crash in my head. It actually hurt just a bit, sort of like brain freeze after guzzling down half of a Slurpee in one gulp.

"I was summoned here," Blodwen answered, giving Claude a sideways glance, "by somebody that knew the ancient rites. Any faerie can be called upon by somebody of the old blood."

*Mystify called her*, Adrianna spoke up sounding strangely out of breath.

*If that is true…then he is*—I thought, but Adrianna cut me off.

*At least part faerie.*

I'd noticed something peculiar about him when we'd first

met. He had freaky second eyelids and there were those bumps or knobs on his back.

"Alright!" I held up my hands. "Everybody needs to stop talking, stop doing anything. There is so much going on, and I think all of us might have a little part of the puzzle bouncing around in our brains."

"What puzzle?" Blodwen asked with a raised eyebrow.

"Let's start with you," I said. "You say that somebody of the blood called you here. When…and more importantly…who?"

"The when is easy," Blodwen answered. "It was six days ago. As far as whom, it was a lesser faerie, but they knew to call me by name."

"So why did it take you almost a week to get here?"

"There was business to attend to after the disaster that you created by assassinating Prince Fraylee. As you recall, I told you to stay out of it. Did you expect me to fly in on a broom, or just drop what I am doing because of a summoning? What am I, some sort of demon?" the woman asked with an amused, if not somewhat condescending, chuckle.

I still was not sure which of these guises was real, but I doubted that I would like her in either one. She just seemed so—

*She's a real bitch*, Adrianna finished my thought. *But I think you need to know something.*

*Is now really the time?* I asked.

*I have subdued Mystify.*

"I have heard that ghouls are able to lock themselves away in a part of their mind to avoid feeling pain," Blodwen was suddenly right in my face. Of course she had to lean down just a bit to do so seeing as she was now almost six feet tall in her current "Venus" form. "You seem to do that quite often. Almost like you are slipping away to a world of your own. And…" Her eyes grew wide and I thought for a second that she was trying to maybe hypnotize me with her big, blue, glowing orbs. "You smell of…*kindred*!" That last word was a whisper that was barely a whisper.

"Okay…I am gonna quote that blond girl from *Shaun of the Dead*. Everybody just calm…the fuck…DOWN!" I don't really like to swear. I had a teacher that used to say something to the effect of "If you can't think of something more original than profanity...perhaps you should not speak at all." Personally, I think that if you seldom swear, doing so has a much greater impact. People are so jolted by it that they are shocked into silence. Also, I broadcast that just a forcefully into my head as I did out loud.

I spun to face my little pack of minions. They had been strangely silent and well-behaved during all of this. I didn't know whether it was due to fascination, or if it might simply be that the combined presence of Claude, Blodwen, and perhaps even me, was enough to keep them quiet.

"All of you back to your rooms." I was more than a little surprised when there was not one single protest, especially from the goblins. They always had something to say when you tried to tell them what to do.

I looked down at Claude, making a very serious effort not to be a gushy, drooling idiot. "I think we start with you."

"I can appreciate that you have made an attempt to assume control, but the fact remains that you are a guest in my home. I do not believe that you will be telling me what to do in my house, love." Claude rose to his feet and was busy dusting himself off and trying to pretend that he had not just come within one more big squeeze of being crushed into jelly by an owlbear.

"Love?" I snorted. "Don't try to play like you are all suave and sophisticated. And you might try thanking me instead of acting like a creep. If not for me, Theodore would have squeezed you like a set of bagpipes. And as for being a guest in your home! Do you make it a habit to lock all of your guests in a dungeon?"

"And just where would you have me invite you to stay during the day? This house is designed to allow maximum sunlight in every room. Unless I have been seriously misled, that would have left you in a very unpleasant situation. I did not have any place that I could keep you during the day with the exception of this one peculiar bathroom that reminds me more of a cross between a cess pool and a swamp." He gave a tug to the poofy sleeves of his silk shirt and flicked the collar with his index finger and thumb. "And you are correct in saying that it would be proper for me to extend a thanks for calling off that owlbear. I had no idea one of those was down here."

"You had no idea?" I scoffed. "You have all these poor creatures locked away down here like animals. Granted, goblins might be foul, vile little creatures, but what gives you the right to have them all locked up?"

"I had been assured by the floor maiden that things were just fine down here, and that there was no rush. I could get the affairs of the estate in order during these first few days and then deal with the supplicants."

"Supplicants?" I was confused, but a tiny kernel of WTF was starting to sprout.

"I was informed that several creatures form the surrounding area had come to offer services to the new Psychic."

"That lying little bitch!" I snarled.

I hated being played for a fool. I mean really, I did a good enough job on my own of looking like a fool, the last thing that I needed was somebody "helping" me.

"If you two will excuse me for just a moment," I said, raising a silencing finger at both Blodwen and Claude when they both opened their mouths in what was probably going to be some sort of protest.

Turning on a heel, I stalked back down the corridor. I stopped at the door and took a deep breath. If I was right—and I was honestly hoping that I was not—then I had been duped worse than a teenage girl on a used car lot.

"Gretch?" I called as I opened the door.

There was a sucking noise sort of like when you get a foot stuck in the mud and lose your shoe when you pull it free. I peeked in to discover the mud troll on the far side of the room. She was standing beside a solid partition and was looking over her shoulder at me. All of the tears streaks and that timid countenance were gone. It was replaced by eyes that dripped hatred.

"I thought ghouls to be so much smarter...clever...and far less gullible," Gretch said in a voice that matched the hatred in her eyes. "Such a disappointment."

"Yeah…you and my mom can share notes," I shot back.

"Did you really think that I could be so pathetic…so weak?" Gretch asked in absolute sincerity. "Are you really so naïve to our world?"

"Apparently."

"Then that should make this so much easier."

"Make what easier?" I asked, hoping for the typical evil villain monolog. I wasn't quite sure that Gretch was the evil villain, but she was certainly on their team.

"The war, you stupid ghoul." Gretch actually turned to face me. I might have been imagining things, but she seemed to have grown taller. "All we need to do is remove a few obstacles and then it will be open season on…*your* type."

Here we go again. "My type? You mean ghouls?"

"All of the undead. You are all abominations and have no place on this earth. Ghouls were supposed to have been obliterated centuries ago. The Templars failed the first time by not ensuring that they had hunted you to extinction. That will not be a mistake that is repeated."

"You know," I took another step into the room and closed the door behind me so that I had the exit blocked, "I liked you a lot better before."

"You mean when I was a pathetic, blubbering fool? When I was perhaps a shade weaker than you? When I was something that you could pity and feel superior over?"

"Actually, I was thinking that I liked you more when you weren't such a bitch." I hated what had to be done, but I had a feeling that my options were limited. I willed my fingers to extend to the razor sharp claws.

I advanced on the mud troll. A flicker of fear replaced the hatred, but, to her credit, Gretch bared her dark brown fangs. Huh…I hadn't noticed those before.

She opened her mouth and let loose with a slurry of stinking black mud. The type that you can't even seem to scrape off with a stick. It hit me like the blast from a fire hose and slammed me up against the wall. I felt the thick gloopy stuff fill my mouth and nose. Thankfully I had no real need to breathe or I might have been in trouble. Notice that I did not say "panic"? Yeah…that's because I went ballistic. My toes switched and Sharkmouth came. The bad thing about that was that I had inadvertently just provided Gretch with a bigger target.

Thankfully the mud spew stopped. I wiped at my eyes with the back of my hands. Strange how instinct kicks in. It was like the ghoul part of me had come alive. The human Ava would have sliced her face to ribbons without thinking to reverse my palms out. Also, it seemed that my super senses were suddenly back in a rush.

I heard a wet squishing sound coming closer. It was no problem pinpointing just where the sound originated, and I timed it with as much perfection as a person robbed of actual sight could. One hand slashed out and I heard a screeching wail.

"You will pay for that, ghoul!" Gretch bubbled. Either she was turning into a mud puddle or I'd scored a nice hit. Either way, I tensed for the next attack and was rewarded with a solid blow that sent me tumbling to the floor.

"Is that all you got?" I growled as I was finally able to see…mostly. I mean, things were a bit blurry, but for the most part I could at least make out shapes.

One shape in particular was charging me. Maybe it was a trick of my blurred vision, but it looked like both arms had risen up and then melded to become one big sort of club-like thing. *That might hurt*, I thought, and timed a diving roll just as it came down with a thunderous splat that shook the floor.

I came up to my knees and spun with a backhand. I felt the claws of my right hand sink into something with the consistency of melty ice cream. There was another roar and that club appendage whirled and came down hard on my arm. I think I heard a crunch, but I had already cranked up that 80s metal playlist. The real Van Halen was taking me on a trip down *Mean Street*. Didn't Eddie have just the sweetest smile?

I had ended up skidding across the floor somehow and was now sort of on my side and almost wedged under the bed. The 'squish-slurrp' of mud troll feet were coming at what sounded like a run. I would not be able to get to my feet in time…so I decided to use them as a weapon. I waited until one short, thick, stubby leg was close enough, and I kicked out as hard as I could. This time I scored a good hit. I know this because part of the mud troll went one way and part of her went another. The scream was epic and rivalled the screeching wail of Diamond Dave at his best.

Gretch fell hard and wet. There was a gush of mud from what I could only imagine to be the stump of the severed leg, and then a sound like a water balloon landing on a sidewalk. Mud went everywhere. All that remained of the mud troll was a brown slurry of goop that smelled like rotten swamp gas.

*Nooooo!* a voice wailed in my head loud enough to stagger me.

*Mystify?* I reached out tentatively.

*Ava, I need you to trust me,* Adrianna's voice came in a rush. *I need you to release me from any bonds for a moment.*

*One thing at a time,* I snapped. Strange, but I felt Cody trying to hide.

*No time, I need you to do it now if you don't want to—*

Silence. But that wasn't exactly right. There was a feeling of…absence.

## 9

# Goodbye to You

*Adrianna?* I asked inwardly.

There was nothing but my own mind. I climbed to my feet and looked around. It looked like somebody had dumped a hundred gallons of chunky chocolate pudding in a giant blender and then turned it on without a lid in place.

The pain in my arm was bad, but nothing I could not get past. I just had to remember one very important thing: don't look at the arm! It was like I had two extra elbow joints between my actual elbow and my wrist.

*Hey, lady?* I heard Cody's voice. It sounded distant, but more than that, it sounded scared.

*Cody? Where are Mystify and Adrianna?*

I needed to get back out there and deal with Claude and Blodwen, but this was sort of important seeing as how it was inside my head. I had no idea what kind of impact this could have on me.

*I don't know where they are, but it is suddenly really trippy in here.*

I focused all my attention on finding Adrianna. It was like finding a needle in a stack of needles. Yeah…you heard me correctly. An idea came suddenly and with such clarity that I could not dismiss it. I focused on the memory of that first time I had taken a nibble of The Queen of the Zombies. It had been during our little graveyard showdown.

I could feel a line of drool almost escape from the corner of my mouth as I recalled just how yummy she tasted to me. In a flash, it was almost like I was falling inside my own head. I adjusted a little and changed my fall into flight. It isn't really falling until you hit the ground. Granddaddy always said that it wasn't the fall that killed you, but the sudden stop at the end.

*You never cease to surprise me*, Adrianna whispered. It was strange, but I swear she was standing right behind me and whispering those words into my ear. I could almost feel her breath on the back of my neck.

*Do what needs to be done*, I managed after I shook off the oddly pleasant and unnaturally sexual rush I was feeling. I looked around. I could still see the mud troll's room, but it was like I was seeing the room through a veil. I mean, I was still standing in it, but...I wasn't.

*Fool!* a voice thundered. It was Mystify, and he was the perfect cure for the tingle that Adrianna had just sent through me.

*Whoa! How did you get in here? I thought we were in your head or something?* Cody chimed in.

I remember watching *Alice in Wonderland* when I was a kid. That was the closest that I could come to describing this experience. I had fallen down the rabbit hole.

There was a shower of sparks from nowhere that quickly fizzled and then changed to moths which subsequently burst into flame and became nothing more than black ash. I felt the ash begin to dissolve, and with it...any trace of Mystify.

If you think you are spinning, you should be me. This was worse than the time that I experimented with acid and watched Pink Floyd's *The Wall*.

There was a fading scream and a roar that echoed while still sounding like it was muffled behind a wall of pillows. Another burst of energy ricocheted past and vanished with the very last of the ash. Then...silence.

I waited a few heartbeats and still heard nothing. Then, from everywhere and nowhere, I heard Cody. *Duuu-uu-uude!*

*Great, I have Bill or Ted in here.*

*Huh? My name is Cody.*

I was about to say something when I suddenly felt as if I was spiraling out. There was a pop like when you hold your nose and blow to clear your ears.

In a blast of cool air...everything was...normal? I looked around and nothing had really changed. The veil was gone and things were just as they had been.

"What the hell was that?" I asked out loud.

*Perhaps I have grossly underestimated you*, Adrianna said with what sounded like respect.

"I doubt it," I replied, again not bothering to keep that internal.

*I honestly did not believe that you would be able to get in here. That requires a degree of concentration that few can manage.*

"Then you are gonna feel even sillier when I ask you what the heck you are talking about?" I huffed. I could feel Adrianna's amazement. That was not something that I was used to getting from The Queen of the Zombies.

"Is everything okay in there, Ava?" Claude's voice came from outside the room.

*We will discuss this later, Ava*, Adrianna said. And then the strangest thing happened; she and Cody were suddenly locked away and I had my mind to myself. Mystify was gone. Not just missing or unable to be found. He was totally gone.

"Everything is fi-*aarrch-yow*!" I yelped as I opened the door. I felt a tinge of pain and realized that I had just grabbed the door and opened it with my broken arm.

Claude jumped back like he thought that I might attack him. Blodwen had retreated to the entrance and was peering down from the top step. She had resumed the old crone form again.

"You have slain a mud troll," the detached and spider like voice hissed, but it was not angry or accusing. Unless I was totally off base, she sounded surprised and perhaps even impressed.

"It was just a little one," I shrugged. Seriously, I had fought much tougher.

"Yes," Blodwen agreed, "but this one was enchanted and was drawing power from something. There was a ribbon of faerie power swirling around this place that is now gone."

That was obviously something to do with Mystify. I had more than a feeling that he and the mud troll had been in serious cahoots.

"That is all fine and good." I held up my broken arm as if to remind them, although judging by the green tint on Claude's face, I think it was unnecessary. "I need something to eat if I am going to repair…or whatever it is that ghouls do."

"I think we need to get a few things handled *before* we allow the ghoul to mend," Blodwen said with a shift that put her in the middle of the doorway. Seriously, if that hag thought that she was able to stop me from passing, then I had news for her.

I was one those women who was not shy about popping Midol like candy during PMS. Pain and I had nothing to say to each other. And now that I knew of a way to make my boo-boos go bye-bye, I was not about to let some gwyll or faerie—or whatever the heck this woman-thing might be—stop me from obtaining my remedy.

"You will listen to what I have to say before you do anything, *ghoul*!"

I didn't like the way that she said the word "ghoul." In fact, I think it was high time that I start making some changes. From all accounts that I have been given, ghouls are straight up bad asses. So why was I acting like plain old Ava? Why was I allowing these people—

*That is why*, Adrianna scolded. *You continue to look at things like a person. You have no idea of your power or ability. I hate to break it to you, but there was a reason that there was a concentrated effort to wipe ghouls from the face of the earth. You tilt the playing field very dramatically if I may use a term that might make sense to you.*

*But…* I started to argue, only, I had no argument. I was ignorant to this new world and there was no pretending otherwise.

*You just did a Mindwalk,* Adrianna said with undisguised

82

amazement. *And you did it without being told that you could, much less being taught how.*

*Or knowing even slightly what you are talking about,* I added.

"Stop ignoring me, you unholy eater of the dead," Blodwen barked, snapping my focus back to her.

"I think," I let my fingers go switchblade and decided to allow my toes as well since I'd already ruined my shoes, "that you don't really want me to pay you *too* much attention."

Just that quick, Blodwen took a step back. Once again, I noticed that her eyes had flashed to my fingers with very noticeable fear showing in them.

"S-s-stay where you are," Blodwen tried to demand, but it really came out more like a plea than anything else.

A voice in my head was quoting Vinnie Barbarino, *I'm so confused!* One moment, Blodwen was all bluster and in my face, and the next...she was a cowering little old lady.

*It's the claws, Ava,* Adrianna said with smug satisfaction. *The Gwyllion are indeed a very powerful and dangerous member of the faerie family, but they have a fear that borders on phobic when it comes to having a dagger pointed at them. In fact, travelers from their Celtic homeland would never go out at night without a dagger on hand just in case.*

I glanced down at my switchfingers and then over at the cowering crone. *Wow, that was more unsolicited information than I'd ever gotten from either Morgan or Betty*, I thought, but not in such a way (or at least that was my hope) that Adrianna could detect it. It would almost be too weird if The Queen of the Zombies and I became...and I almost don't dare say or think it...friends.

I smiled big and willed my nails to retract. Instantly, Blodwen relaxed. There was a shimmer and she morphed into her Venus form.

"Perhaps we can come to an understanding," I suggested. I made a point of stabbing the goblin cubes that were still scattered about the stairs. It was slow work, but my arm began to mend.

"Despite what you might think," the svelte woman leaned in the doorway and shook her head almost sadly, "there is not likely any solution that you can suggest to bridge the divide between us. You are a ghoul…it is that simple. As a faerie, we are sworn enemies and I do not foresee anything that will cause me to stop seeking your extinction."

A thought hit me and my eyes widened. "But Rain and the other faeries don't seem to have a problem with me," I offered. "In fact, they were in my home just the other day and did not seem the least bit driven to take my life."

"They are of the new generation," Blodwen sighed. "They are ignorant children and have no memories of the terror that *your* type have brought down upon us. If it was not the ghouls, then it was the vampires. Tis more the pity that the Templars did not make any headway on the demise of those bloodsucking parasites from the depth of Hell when they were killing your kind in scores."

"Rain and the others seemed to actually like me, but they sure did not care for Belinda," I muttered.

"Belinda Skaär?" The woman's head popped up and her crystal blue eyes narrowed.

"I don't know," I said with a shrug. "We aren't very close. I have no idea what her last name is."

"Young, blonde, and very full of herself?"

"Well you just described every Playmate bimbo from the Hefner Mansion, but yeah, that could also be my Belinda."

"Yes, well if it is the same vampire, there is good reason that the faeries you know would not have much trust in her. She has fed on more than her fair share of our kind. Unlike ghouls, there are enough vampires still around so that their horrors are more than just legends…they are still etched in our current history. I may be one of the few of my kind that is old enough to remember the sidhe invasions of the ghouls back in what humans call the Dark Ages."

Holy crap! I thought. *Blodwen is one ancient old gal.*

*Ahem,* I heard what sounded like Adrianna clearing her throat.

*Well compared to me she is*, I shot that thought inwardly.

"Listen," I would try reason, "we obviously have some issues between us that need dealing with. If you just let me take care of my arm, then we can sit down and talk this out. I bet you will be surprised that those younger faeries are not the only believers in a new generation and way of doing things."

Blodwen seemed to consider it. Meanwhile, Claude had ducked out at some point. Not that I cared...I mean, he was all Vince Neal sexy, and he really did seem like he was caught in the middle of all of this.

"Nobody will say that I am not at least willing to listen, and with all the pieces of the puzzle dumped out of the box, perhaps it is time to start putting some of the edge pieces together," Blodwen said by way of agreement; at least that was how I was taking her comment.

I stepped out into the hallway and was surprised to find it empty. I looked down the length and every door was shut.

"They heard your fight. None of them wanted to be just standing around when you came out and needed to replenish," Blodwen said in response to my questioning look. "The tales of the ghouls' appetite after battle is a thing of legends."

*That would be the* Fame Rabia, I thought. Oddly enough, the last time I'd experienced it was after that first meeting with the then unseen Blodwen. Actually, she had not done a thing to me, it had been her goblins.

"Can I ask you something?" I moved into step beside Blodwen as we exited the holding area...jail...or whatever this was down here. The faerie gave a shrug that I took as a sign to go ahead. "What is the deal with goblins? I mean, I have been running into the little critters just about everywhere. Only, I never saw anything of the sort in Portland. I've certainly never seen them around Morgan."

"They are...cheap labor. I guess that would be the best way to put it so that you might understand. The goblin is a practically fearless fighter. They breed like rats and litters have been known to number between ten and fifteen at times. A female can give birth every four months and can begin bearing offspring within their first year.

"Their biggest drawback is that they are only as loyal as their last meal. The moment that they sense a shift in power, they will turn on whoever they were in service of and join the individual that they see as the likely victor."

I noticed a slight tone of derision in Blodwen's otherwise silky voice. I really did prefer her in this form and had no idea why she would ever take on that crone visage. But as I was about to allow myself to get comfy with Blodwen's beauty in her Venus form, another thought came.

"The goblins here…they were yours," I said. I shot a look at the woman and saw her lips press tight in annoyance. "They turned on you—"

"And joined you," the woman finished.

"So they must have figured that I was going to come out of this little encounter as the winner."

"They are not always right," Blodwen insisted, but I heard the falseness of that statement ringing just as if she had a neon light above her that flashed the word "LIAR."

"That must really have you pissed," I said while trying to keep any of the amusement that I felt from coming through in my voice. After all, we were almost being civil towards one another at the moment; no sense in spoiling the mood.

"I would say that I am more disappointed."

"Are these the same ones that were doing all of those terrible things to me that day?"

"A few…some. I can never keep them straight. I honestly believe that only a goblin can tell one of their kind from another."

"What about the bugbears?"

"Nope…those were Claude's."

I heard the past tense in that statement. Again, I did not want to press the issue, things were actually feeling like they were calming down. No sense in stirring up the hornets.

"Obviously the goblins sense something coming off you that I do not," Blodwen finally said after we had travelled the length of a long hallway and were about to enter what certainly looked like a large dining room.

Claude was seated at the head of a table long enough to warrant texting during meals. However…he was not alone. Behind him were the three revenants and that swamp ape thingy. If it had been just that, I would say that things were okay and this was just going to be a normal meal…or as normal as one could be when the guests included a gwyll, a Psychic and a ghoul.

Unfortunately, that was not the case. There were two men seated at the table as well. Both were wearing suits that looked like they might cost a few thousand bucks easy. They were also wearing dark shades. That is never a good sign. You can almost always tell that an individual is a villain when they are wearing dark glasses…inside…at night.

"Have a seat, Miss Birch," one of the men said with a voice that was possibly even emptier of emotion than what I usually heard from Morgan. Both stood in unison and placed their hands behind backs almost with military precision and synchronicity.

To quote Rachel Morgan (and I have it on good authority the real Rachel actually says this), "Crap on toast."

Next, on a Very Special *That Ghoul Ava...*

# 10

# Walk Like an Egyptian

"I think I'd rather stand," I said, moving over just enough inside the entry arch so that my back was against the wall.

I scanned the room. I had the way I'd come in, but unless there was some secret passage that I'd missed, that way only led back to the dungeon. Yep, that was what I had decided to call the holding area. The only other way out was on the other side of the room...past the Men in Black.

"Really, Miss Birch, this might take a few minutes and I think you would be much more comfortable if you had a seat," the second man spoke.

I shot a withering look at Claude, who just smiled at me like a puppy that had just fetched a ball for his master. The only problem was that I was pretty sure that I was the ball. I cast a look over at Blodwen and...

*She didn't know*, Adrianna was suddenly front and center.

*And can I safely assume that these are Templars?* I asked her.

*Undoubtedly*, was her response.

"I don't recall being asked if these...*men* could join us," Blodwen said, finally breaking her silence.

"Let's not pretend that we are all shiny, happy people here. You guys are Templars...I am a ghoul. According to the little bit that I know about you guys, you want to wipe out all ghouls. However, I think that somebody has bigger plans, because you've helped fund or maybe even participated in an assault on a faerie sidhe. And let's not even get to the part where you guys have basically hijacked my roommate and best friend." Okay, that last part might not be entirely true, but I was building a head of steam and it felt good to toss about some of the blame that I was carrying around.

I brought on my switchfingers and toes, keeping Shark-mouth in reserve. I doubted that I would be surprising anybody considering how pretty much everybody in the Supernatural community—which I had to include the Templars as a part of in some way—knew more about the various powers and abilities of ghouls than I did.

"You have been misinformed, Miss Birch," the first man spoke. "While it is true that we once sought the extinction of ghouls, we were only doing as we were bid to do at a time where it seemed that perhaps the ghouls might be posing a possible threat to humanity. We have no such interests at this time."

"What?" Blodwen choked.

Hmmm…that was an interesting response. I crossed my arms and gave the gwyll a look that was perhaps a bit more laced with curiosity than actual menace. The way this woman bounced back and forth, she was becoming more difficult to watch than a pair of professional Chinese ping pong players on crack. One minute she was all "DEATH TO GHOULS!" and the next she was acting scared of me, then the next minute she was talking to me like we were girlfriends.

"I don't believe that we have had the pleasure of meeting," the second Man in Black said to Blodwen.

"I am Blodwen Cadwallader, Queen of the Celtic Mulingar Gwyllion, Holder of the Blue Sphere, Cosantóir of the Ten Sidhe," she said with all the regality you can imagine from somebody with so many titles. I noticed she skipped the part about her friends being able to call her "Muffy." I guess she didn't want to be friends with the Templars.

"Yes, we are aware of who you are, and it is our honor and

privilege to meet you, your highness," the two men said in a creepy-twin sort of unison.

"We had no idea that you had ventured over to our side of the pond," the first man said as he made a slight bow. "And I would love some time to chat if you will grant it, but I am afraid that I must speak with Miss Birch. It is of utmost importance."

I gave this guy a closer look. The first thing that stood out was his near absence of a smell. I would imagine that he was a human. And I had learned from Lisa that they get a ring that apparently slows their aging almost entirely. However, it was not complete because I could get at least a hint of that smell humans all share—the smell of impending death. He had dark hair, almost black, which complimented his darker complexion that belied either Italian or Spanish. His eyes were a mystery since they were well hidden behind those solid black glasses. He had some pretty full lips for a guy, and I had to quash any thoughts of what it must be like to kiss them. He had broad shoulders that gave the impression that he could totally rock a tight tee-shirt. His waist was not exactly slim, but there was an appealing taper from chest to the beltline.

I looked at the second guy and was only mildly surprised to discover that he was almost undistinguishable from his partner. They were sporting more similarities than differences. Still, the first man had something about him that dripped raw attractive sexuality.

"So, you seem to know my name, but I got no idea what to call you guys unless I go with Thing One and Thing Two," I said, directing my statement at the second man just because the first one was starting to make me tingle in my tummy. I did not need that kind of distraction at the moment.

"My name is Gordon Wasserman and my partner is Race Mitchell," Man in Black Number Two said.

*Race Mitchell?* That name jingled something in my memory. I knew it from somewhere, but was drawing a total blank until Adrianna spoke up.

*He is connected to Lisa. In fact, he is one of the men who has come to your house on a few occasions when Lisa would put you in stasis*, Adrianna said.

Just like that, I remembered when I had heard that name. He was not just connected to Lisa. She had said that this man in particular was her mentor. He was not just some random Templar.

If I was guarding myself before, I was on full alert now. This man had some 'splainin' to do. It took all of my willpower not to launch myself at him and start demanding answers.

"Easy, Miss Birch," Race cautioned. He did not move or make any threatening gesture, but there was menace ringing clear in his voice.

"You and I got some issues to clear up," I said with as much calm as I could maintain. I did not want this guy to know that he had turned me into a seething cauldron of emotion. Besides, he was really cute, and I was having a hard time hating him as much as I probably should.

*This is no time to be thinking with your loins*, Adrianna scolded.

*Loins? Seriously?*

I shoved Adrianna into her box and made an extra effort to ensure that she stayed there. I did not need to be distracted at the moment. I checked and was not all that surprised to discover that Cody was sealed off.

I took a deep breath. I was in a dining room with some sort of Celtic faerie queen, the Dallas, Texas Psychic, a trio of revenants, a swamp ape, and two Templars—one of whom was supposedly Lisa's mentor.

I walked to the table, ignoring Blodwen as she shied away from me when I passed. Seriously, was she that scared of my claws? Pulling out a chair, I sat down, retracting all of my finger and toe blades.

"You get five minutes. If I don't like what I hear, then I will probably start shredding people. Honestly, I am beyond annoyed, I want to go home, and I will be on a plane tonight one way or the other."

Morgan was going to love that. She had me slated to be gone for three days, but I needed to come home and find Lisa. I had to fix things between us. If I could eat the dead, then how bad would a Super-sized helping of crow hurt?

"I know that you are aware that there has been some division in the community of the Supernaturals. We have reason to believe that a demon has managed to cross the veil—" Race Mitchell began.

"Hold on," I said, bringing a hand up in that universal signal for "halt." I had to be sure that I'd heard him correctly. "A demon? Like from Hell?"

"Yes and no," Race replied with a nod.

I hated when people said that. It can't be yes *and* no. It is either yes *or* no. I waved my hand, indicating for him to continue.

"Demons are not actually from Hell. They are from what you might consider an extra dimension. They were banished by a powerful necromancer a long time ago and the gate that was used remains to this day. The Pyramids of Giza..."

He left that last bit out there for me to digest. Apparently Race was giving me a bit more credit than I deserved. If he was waiting for a response...he was going to be disappointed. After a few heartbeats in which everybody stared at me as if in anticipation, he continued.

"The demons managed to hurl a curse back at the necromancer just before the gate closed. Unbeknownst to the necromancer, his DNA had been altered. He was slowly driven mad by nightmares and eventually took his life. It took him almost two weeks to free himself from his tomb, and when he did, he found that he craved dead flesh. He eventually drowned or simply vanished in what is now known as the Dead Sea."

"You have got to be kidding!" I blurted.

"Has nobody told you of the origins of the ghoul?" Race asked with genuine astonishment.

"Nobody has told me a damn thing," I snapped. I was tempted to call Adrianna forth. I bet she could be helpful right now, but I wanted to figure this out on my own. "Please...continue."

I saw a look pass between Race and Gordon. Gordon shrugged and, with a nod, Race continued with his history lesson.

"The necromancer became what you would consider to be a

carrier. The magic of the curse that swirled within him actually seeped from his body. It was transferred to others.

"It took years...decades in some cases. But, over time, people that the curse found purchase in would return. However, it was a very rare occurrence and it took over a thousand years for the ghouls to grow in number.

"According to legend, a Greek mystic figured out that this curse could only be realized at its full potential if a person took his own life, and then only after he returned from the dead and discovered himself to be a ghoul. He reportedly began to harvest the children that he had sired from his slaves and created what would be considered a cult by today's standards.

"All of those children were sent in to impregnate his female slaves. Once they reached an age, these children would willingly take their lives and then rise again as ghouls. Only, it was not a hundred percent. In fact, if you can believe the scrolls, it only expressed itself in one in three.

"Still, over the period of several hundred years, an army was born...literally. During the rise of the Roman Empire, the ghouls were a force to be reckoned with. Of course they loved war...it provided them with an endless food supply.

"When the Romans moved into what is now considered the UK, the ghouls encountered the faeries for the first time. Somehow, they discovered that they became almost invincible after consuming the fey. We have no idea how this came to pass or if it is even true, but the ghouls changed during this time. There is speculation that it had something to do with faerie blood. However, it was also around that time that ghouls began to go mad and started killing indiscriminately."

I thought about how I had learned a few things from Adrianna. Consuming her had transferred some of her abilities to me. Plus, I had her in my head. I tried to imagine what that sort of thing would have done to somebody from such a long time ago. Superstitions and the unknown were a much darker part of things back then. Also, I had never eaten a faerie. I wondered how that might differ.

That was when I made my first connection. Sure, it might

seem like no big deal, and you might even be surprised that I just made the connection, but I had eaten plenty of dead people. None of them were in my head or had given me any sorts of powers. This only happened when I ate a Supernatural being!

"...when the Templars were formed. Of course they were only known as The Brotherhood back then. They would not be known as Templars for hundreds of years when the Holy Roman Church conscripted them."

Ooops, I was missing stuff. I could ponder later. Lately I had been getting better at controlling my trips to Ava Land. It was like any other power. This one was part of how a ghoul was able to withstand and ignore pain. Boredom can be painful; that is my only explanation for some of my earlier moments in some of my previous adventures where I slipped into my mind and would miss things when people were talking to me.

"Still, those first men all made an oath to the Queen Mother in the sidhe. As you may know, an oath made in a sidhe binds the person to it...be they human or otherwise. And so those first men rode forth.

"They sought the ghouls and chased them all around Europe and parts of Northern Africa. It was during those travels that they began to encounter other beings of the Supernatural world—" Race was saying almost as if this were some sort of practiced speech that he had given before. Honestly, I was not even remotely interested.

"Okay!" I snapped, cutting him off. "Thanks for the history lecture, but I just want to know why you are here and what any of this has to do with me."

"That makes two of us," Blodwen mumbled. I am pretty sure she did it so low that I was the only one in the room that heard.

"You are a woman," Race said simply.

"Thanks for noticing," I replied after a moment of silence. Apparently that was supposed to mean something.

"You are kidding me," Blodwen breathed. She shot me a look that had me suddenly feeling extremely self-conscious.

"The curse that was given is passed on through what is now called genetics. It is hereditary," Race said when it was clear that

I was clueless. "But it was only transferred to men...or at least that was the case until Boudicca..."

When were people going to get it through their heads? Just because you say something with all the certainty and enthusiasm that comes from your education and upbringing, that does not mean that those around you have any idea what you are talking about.

It is like you men and your sports. You blabber on about meaningless things when whatever game you are watching is on...pass interference...holding...strike zones...double-dribbles. Umm, I got news for you, most of us ladies just see guys with amazing butts in tight pants doing a lot of bending over.

"Okay, I'll bite. Who is Boudicca?" I finally asked.

"She became the first female ghoul known in history. And until you...the *only* female ghoul," Race answered. "Before that, she had been perhaps one of the fiercest warriors to ever confront Nero and his Romans. To avoid capture when it was clear that she was finally about to be defeated by the armies of Roman governor, Gaius Suetonius Paulinus, she took her life.

"She awoke to her new life as a ghoul and many believe that it was she that pushed the rebellion in Gaul that led to Nero's downfall and eventual death by suicide. Apparently somebody had convinced the Roman emperor that he would return with amazing power if he took his own life."

"And so what happened to her? I mean, she sounds like way more of a badass than I will ever be." I was actually becoming curious. This Boudicca sounded like one tough chick.

"The male ghouls turned on her and destroyed her," Race answered. "They made an agreement with the Queen Mother of all faeries and the Templars after Boudicca apparently single-handedly wiped out an entire sidhe and took it as her own residence. In exchange for their lives and the geas to eliminate all ghouls that had been placed on the Templars being removed, they agreed to kill her."

# 11

## You Dropped a Bomb On Me

"Wait...what?" I sputtered.

"The males had discovered that they could gain small bits of the powers from any Supernatural that they consumed, only, it was for a very short time," Blodwen spoke up. "However, Boudicca did not seem to lose her gained abilities. The reason that she had been able to enter the sidhe in the first place was because she had eaten a faerie from that sidhe. This meant that all she needed to do to enter a sidhe was to find and eat one of its members. The moment that she did, she would not only know of its location, but she would be able to enter without any of the defenses causing her harm.

"The male ghouls vowed in the presence of the sidhe that they would never again attack the faeries if they were spared," Blodwen replied.

"It is believed that there is something genetic in the female ghoul that grants her the ability to permanently absorb the powers of any Supernatural that she consumes," Race said, giving me a very hard stare.

I heard a slight gasp and saw that Claude was looking at me with a new level of interest. If he knew that I had consumed Mystify, then what might he be thinking? And if Adrianna wiped him out, or whatever it is that she did, then are his powers still floating in my being? Whoa! Another thought bloomed! Does that make me basically the same as a Psychic?

So much was swirling in my head. It was dizzying. I did not think that I was prepared to take that on all by myself. As crazy as it was, I needed some help.

*Adrianna?* God, even in my mind I sounded pitiful.

*Yes, Ava?* The woman was instantly right there in response.

*When I have you...locked up, can you still hear what is going on around me?*

*No. I can sense when your feelings or emotions change, but I can't actually hear anything, including what you say.*

Of course she could be lying through her teeth, but I could *sense* that she was being truthful. Hmm...that was nifty. This was better than the ju-ju.

*Well, I need you to hang out. There is some stuff being said and I think I might need your help.* I sensed her grow just a bit pleased with herself. Great! Well, I could deal with that later. Right now I had to get my mind—*our* mind—wrapped around this latest revelation.

"I don't imagine that you would be wanting to share information on any Supernatural beings that you have consumed?" Race asked. The look on his face said that he might have asked that question once and was repeating himself.

"I don't know you well enough to tell you my favorite color," I replied, making my way to the table. Maybe I would sit down. It looked like this might take a moment or two, and I was going to try and use this for my own gain just like I knew that these Templars were trying to do.

"Okay...how about a trade," Race offered. I saw Gordon shoot him an almost angry look.

"You mean information?" I pulled out the chair and sat directly across from Race Mitchell. He was even cuter up close. Bad, Ava! Keep your head in the game, girl.

*Yes, you do not want to make a mistake around Templars,* Adrianna warned. *And no matter what you agree to, I don't think you should mention me in any way.*

"How about I start?" Race folded his hands and leaned forward and removed his dark shades.

Yikes, he has got some very appealing eyes. They were a chocolate brown and his dark lashes were the kind women spent hours trying to create with expensive mascara. Also, he has that radiating confidence thing. You ladies know exactly what I am talking about, don't you. Some guys just have that thing where you know that they are not even aware that rejection is a possibility. These are the guys who don't even think of *not* coming up to you in a bar and saying hello and then actually starting a conversation that does consist of five poorly strung together pick-up lines.

He was wearing a well-tailored black suit, but unlike his partner, or whatever Gordon was, Race was not wearing a black tie. His was a blood red with what looked like real spun gold stitching. It rested in the rather impressive and noticeable cleft of his chest.

"Lisa Jenkins." That name shot through my blooming fantasy about Race scooping me into his arms and kissing me in that way that made all of my toes curl tight. And, fellas, that is a real thing that happens.

"What about her?" I tried to sound casual.

"You know very well that she is my plebe."

"Umm…" I really didn't want him to know that I was a total idiot.

*Plebe is basically a word for a military trainee*, Adrianna offered quickly. I did not have any idea where this helpful attitude was coming from, but I was not about to look a gift horse in the mouth.

"And you might be interested to know that she is doing exceptionally well in her training," Race continued. Whether it was to cover my apparent ignorance or to simply move this conversation forward. I was having a very difficult time not wanting to *really* like this guy. "She is in Italy at the moment, but is expected to return in the next day or two. I have sadly lost track of time in all of the hubbub."

Hubbub? Who says that anymore? "And you think that is enough to get me to just spill things?" I asked after Adrianna prompted me.

"Not at all, but I simply thought that might be something that you would like to know."

He wasn't wrong. I was curious as to what the heck she was doing in Italy, but one thing at a time. I shifted in my chair just a bit and leaned back in what I hoped was a confident pose. Just as I got comfy in the overstuffed chair, I felt a strange tingle. It was like a thought that was trying to come to the surface...but different. I shoved it away; now was not the time for my mind to be wandering.

"It is, and thank you." I flashed what I considered to be my friendliest smile. "However, let's hear what you think might be something that would make me want to talk to you. And as for trust, I think that is off the table for—"

Claude jumped to his feet. "If you will all please excuse me for a moment." Without waiting for any sort of acknowledgement, he hurried from the room.

One of the revenants scuttled after him. I felt my mouth purse in that way it would do back when I was a human and had just stepped in a pile of doggie doo while perhaps walking through the park or, even worse, along the beach at the coast. Seriously...I love dogs. But if you can't pick up after them...maybe you need to stick to cats. Or fish.

The tingle was getting stronger, and there was something about it that was starting to really bother me. There was something...*familiar*? I shoved it away again and returned my attention to Race.

"So here is what I offer in the way of information. You can choose if it is worth telling me anything in return. If you do not, then we will part ways here and now." Gordon leaned over and whispered something, to which Race nodded and looked over at Blodwen. "But we would certainly like to speak with you before we leave if you would grant us that favor."

I glanced over and was surprised to discover that she had reverted to her crone form. Seriously? Did she not see the amazing specimen of man sitting across the table? Not that I was interested or anything. I mean, he's a Templar for crying out loud, but still…

"There is a group of former Templars that have discovered that you exist. They want you dead." Race said that like he might be reading the box scores. And yes, I know what that sounds like, my dad used to do it every morning at breakfast…well…until he left us. "They were involved with Prince Fraylee and had plans to raise an army of the offspring created by faeries and goblins. Within a year, they would have been powerful enough to actually launch an attack on humanity.

"For the past few hundred years, there has been an effort to stockpile weapons. From what we have learned, bringing the faeries into play was a strategic move that would allow these renegades a place to retreat to that would basically be impenetrable by anything that the humans countered with.

"They would be able to venture out, launching an attack with a variety of monsters that would paralyze humans. Imagine the horror that would come from seeing jötunn stomping down the middle of Disneyland…or a hundred bugbears loose in a school yard. These were just some of the plans that were on the table according to our sources.

"The plan was *not* to hit military targets, but instead, they were going for massive emotional damage. They would hit the defenseless with a ferocity that would have overwhelmed the general public."

That sounded pretty serious. I still didn't know what any of this had to do with me other than I had killed Prince Fraylee and Merriette. Those two were obviously at the core of whatever plan had been brewing.

"The fact that you are a ghoul and a female makes you sort of like the atomic bomb back in World War Two. The first person to obtain you would be in a position of power. And to eliminate you…well, that would simply take your potential off the table."

Race leaned back in his chair and gave me a look that made me feel like I was under a microscope. It was like he was peeling away parts of me and deciding what to keep and what to toss. I didn't like it one bit.

"First off," I kept my voice calm, "I am not anybody's toy or weapon…or whatever. I might not be a human anymore, but I still have the same feelings and beliefs I had before I became…this!" I rolled my hands and pointed to my face.

"But you are still a ghoul. And even more important, you are a female. You possess amazing power that, if harnessed, could turn you into something unstoppable. If the rumors are true, and you can indeed absorb the powers of the Supernaturals that you consume…well…"

"I would be a Supernatural Swiss Army knife," I muttered.

"That is an interesting analogy, but it is not too far off," Race agreed. "Imagine…all you would need to do is to consume a faerie and you would have access to the sidhe of that particular stronghold. Once inside, you could invite others…and if you were to consume the Godmother of the Sidhe, then you would wield power over all who resided within.

"You were the last piece of a puzzle that was a century in the making. Apparently there was a plan to have you eat Merriette and force all the faeries of that sidhe to breed with a goblin tribe. Prince Fraylee ruined all of that by trying to kill you. It seems that he and Merriette had decided to double-cross the Templar renegade that they had been planning this with and the two had begun the process of breeding mutations on their own."

For the first time, I think I understood what was meant when I kept being told that I think like a human. I understood mortality. For the Supernaturals, life is not the day-to-day grid. Lifespans are measured in centuries. Weeks and months mean nothing. And by some strange coincidence, I had shown up just as some master plan had rolled into motion.

"I am going to give you an honest answer," I finally said with a sigh. "But I do have one silly question. Besides the Fiery Jötunn and the bugbears, what other sorts of freaks can they create?"

"According to all the books, they can produce the two you mentioned as well as kuatons—think *Creature from the Black Lagoon*—and a winged horror called an arachnet which is basically a flying spider with a foot long stinger."

I shuddered. Spiders were bad enough…but ones that flew? That was enough to make my gray skin pebble up in goose bumps.

"And they just thought that I was going to go along with this plan?" I asked. "What would make me want to do such a thing?"

"I will answer you, but you need to give me something first," Race said with a shake of his head. "I think that I have given you a lot of information and deserve something in return."

He was right. Despite the fact that most of it had slid off me and made next to no sense, he had still told me more than anybody else up to this point. That had me wondering how much of this Morgan knew.

"Ava!" a strangled voice that I did not recognize at first cried out from the archway that Claude had vanished through just moments ago.

Well, it looked like I was about to get an answer to that last question. Morgan was in the archway, but I would not have recognized her unless I'd just been thinking of her. She was bloody, beaten, and her face was so swollen that you could not see her eyes. They had been reduced to a pair of bulges with ugly slits. Standing behind her was a trio of bugbears.

I was no expert, but that did not seem like enough to take down Morgan. I mean, if you are a Psychic, you are more than likely some sort of badass…right? I doubted that her only super power was being a total bitch.

"It seems that we have an uninvited guest," Claude said with a sneer that looked totally wrong on that Vince Neal face. He was too pretty to pass himself off as tough.

Then there was a slight rumble. The bugbears shoved Morgan forward and made room for whatever was coming up from behind them. I now had my answer as to how big those fiery jötunn children back home might get if they reached maturity.

Next, on a Very Special *That Ghoul Ava...*

# 12

## Burning Down the House

"Morgan?" I said as I brought my fingers, toes, and even Sharkmouth on. "What are you doing here?"

"T-t-trap…A-Ava…" she managed through lips that look like she had kissed her blender while it was set on high.

"I figured out that much," I muttered.

"Tell them who you ate," Claude said with a smugness that made no sense.

"S-s-say nothing," Morgan managed. The giant backhanded her and sent her flying into a wall. Two revenants scurried over and scooped her up, shoving her into the waiting arms of a bug-bear.

Why wasn't she doing anything? Couldn't she fight back? Surely she had some form of defense.

Ducking to enter through the arch that was easily twenty feet high, the red-skinned monstrosity entered. The creature made a huffing noise that might be a chuckle as he spied me.

I pushed back from the table in an involuntary action that came from my desire to be farther away from this behemoth. He was decked out in some impressive armor. His shin guards looked like the fronts of a pair of cast iron wood stoves. He wore what looked to me like a giant catcher's mitts made from steel wool. They all were glowing red, and I could see the waves of

105

heat rising from them. His chest plate was a massive slab of metal that looked like it would take an entire NFL offensive line to lift. It was rough, and what looked like diamonds glittered from the ornate and peculiar pattern carved in the surface. Then there was the helmet. I did not want to know what creature's skull it was that had been dipped in some sort of shiny metal to be given a silvery look. Heck, maybe it was silver. Overall, this was some serious and impressive armor.

"Die, ghoul! Want to eat gray lady," he said in a voice that sounded like boulders rolling down a mountain.

Hmm…no surprise there. Any time something nasty showed up, it usually wanted to kill me. At least that is how it seemed lately.

"What is the meaning of this, Claude!" an inhuman voice challenged.

My neck almost snapped when I spun to find Blodwen standing beside me. She was still in the crone form, but there was a blue-green hue surrounding her, and her hands were fashioning what looked like an electric blue snowball in between them.

I heard a crash, and my head came around again to Gordon and Race. Both men had shoved their chairs away and drawn what looked like pistol-sized crossbows. I didn't see what damage those tiny darts would do to something as big as that giant. But what did I know? They were Templars. Suddenly I was feeling like the proverbial knife at a gunfight.

"Speak!" Claude barked.

"I'm not a dog," I shot back.

I think I heard something that might have been a laugh escape Morgan's tattered lips. It was hard to tell, and then she coughed up a wad of thick blood and there was no denying the moan of pain.

"Tell them who resides within you, ghoul," Claude demanded.

He gave a nod and the giant brought up one hand, bringing it down on Morgan with a sickening crunch. If she would have been human, she would have been flattened…turned into nothing more than a pulpy smear on the carved rock floor.

Instead, she was now on the ground. But I could see movement. Whether it was breathing or just her trying to get to her feet, it still came with a pained whimper.

"What is your problem?" I growled at Claude.

"I will have her arms and legs ripped from their sockets if you don't speak," Claude said, ignoring my question.

"Why?" I asked, my voice sounding strangely unemotional. Inside I was actually feeling awful. Morgan was being ground into hamburger. Sure, it wasn't like she and I were pals, but I did not like torture, and that was exactly what this was.

"Morgan is *your* Psychic...I think it is self-explanatory," Claude retorted.

Again I am pretty sure that wet, sickly sound I heard from that bloody lump of flesh was a laugh. How Morgan could find anything funny at the moment was beyond me.

*You are not Morgan's ghoul*, Adrianna spoke up. *But he thinks that you are. If a Psychic kills another, all bonds are passed on to the victor. The binding ties that a Psychic has established with any of their subjects go to the surviving Psychic.*

Now it was my turn to laugh. I have no idea what it looks like when I am rocking the Sharkmouth, but judging by the staggering step back that Claude took, I imagine that it was pretty nasty.

"Destroy the ghoul," Claude said to the monstrosity.

The giant charged and was promptly hit in the center of the chest by the blue ball of whatever Blodwen had been holding. Sparks of what looked like electric ice arced across the breastplate. If the jötunn felt anything, it didn't show. In two steps he was on me.

I dove all too easily under his big swipe. I soon discovered that it was too easy for a reason when the backhand caught me. Somehow, I was now on the other side of the room beside a fireplace that could act as a garage for my Corvette. On the plus side of things, the giant was all the way across the room from me now. On the bad side...my right arm did not want to do anything that I told it to do. I had barely healed from that last bit of damage. This was really starting to piss me off.

I had a boyfriend my junior year that had a favorite movie.

We've all had one, right, ladies? That boyfriend who is way too obsessed with a movie to the point where not only does he practically force you to watch it, but he also sits beside you and recites the lines...and not in that cool *Rocky Horror Picture Show* way. Anyway, this one guy was absolutely consumed by a mediocre movie called *The Warriors*. I won't bore you with the plot, but there was this one scene that was actually pretty cool. There was a fight in this park—Central Park probably since the movie is set in New York City. This one gang dressed in baseball uniforms is painted up in a cross between KISS and a crazy clown. There is this music playing during the chase that struck a chord in me for some strange reason. Don't ask me why, but that tune was what I was now hearing in my head.

As I stood, Race and Gordon suddenly jumped into the fight. Templars or not, they didn't stand a chance. Their little dart guns might as well be spit wad straws. To each man's credit, they quickly tossed the pistol-sized crossbows aside and drew swords from under their jackets. I had no idea how they'd managed to conceal them, but each man now held a sword that looked like something from a *Sinbad* movie. The cool Arabian one, not the less-than-funny comedian.

They came from either side in a whirl of steel. The blades crashed on the protective armor of the giant and sent up a burst of sparks that were fitting of a Fourth of July fountain firework. Unfortunately, that was about all they were doing. The giant kicked out with his Yugo-sized foot and sent Gordon through the arch that led back to the dungeon.

Race fared only a teensy bit better. He ducked under the smoking hot mitt that left a vapor trail and came up with a thrust, plunging his blade into the forearm of the giant. And that is where the blade stuck. Yanking its arm up, the giant lifted Race off the ground as the man apparently gripped the hilt of his blade out of reflex.

With the other hand, the giant swatted Race to the floor like a mosquito. I heard the sizzle of flesh and a yelp of pain. Race didn't strike me as the wimpy sort, so if he was expressing pain, I had to think that it hurt. I found out soon enough when the raging giant punted Race's prone figure across the room to a few feet away from me. I could smell his cooked flesh and see huge, angry blisters rising from his face. In fact, one entire cheek looked like a fleshy water balloon.

Before I could catch myself, the first thought that bloomed was, *I bet he won't be nearly as handsome after that. Burn scars are nasty and usually very disfiguring.* I know…pretty shallow, but he had been *so-o* hot.

I turned to fully face the giant and waved Freddy Krueger-style with my good left hand. The giant charged exactly as I had hoped. I'd fought his kind before, and it stood to reason that similar tactics would yield similar results.

I ducked under his swing and tried my own backhanded swipe with my switch-fingered left hand. I scored a hit…but I don't think the big fella noticed. He skidded to a halt and let out a roar that was louder than any concert I'd been to…and I have been to some doozies.

I saw his leg rear back and I waited until the last possible fraction of a second to roll out of the way. When I came up, imagine my surprise when I was standing directly between the legs of my enemy.

*GROSS!*

Adrianna's voice echoed my own as I looked up to discover that giants, or at least this one, did not wear underpants. Like some sort of twisted parody of a penis piñata, hanging right above me were the biggest pair of man berries that I have ever seen in my life. I have already divulged my opinion of the male anatomy. To review: functional if used properly, but not in the slightest bit attractive.

With a single swipe of my only truly still-functional clawed hand, I ended the fight. I had never been a lefty, so my aim was off just a tad, but it did not need to be precise.

I probably should have thought that attack through. Sure, it had produced the desired effect. The giant sort of leaped forward and then came down with a ground shaking thud as he howled in pain, but not before I got drenched in giant blood and conked on the head by a pair of fleshy orbs a bit larger than a basketball.

Yep…giant gonads.

I had to really work hard to push down the feeling of revulsion as well as a slight twinge of sympathy pain, but I knew that I needed to finish this thing off before it got up. Sure, it might not have been able to, but I wasn't about to wait and find out. I ran up onto the downed creature's back and jumped high, coming down with my switch-toes in the back of the giant's neck. With a bit of a twist, the head fell away and hot blood gushed.

I'm not ashamed to say that I carved off a chunk from the dead monster's side and gulped it down. It is so cool…watching my misshapen arm stretch out straight as it mended and healed from the massive break. I took another chunk just to be on the safe side. That was when I heard the anguished cry from my left.

"You must have been very disappointed," I said, pulling Sharkmouth back so that it would not distract from the scene that was about to play out.

Claude narrowed his eyes at me. I could tell he was pissed, and he had been spending more time studying me than anything else since I arrived. I now had a feeling as to why.

"My only question is whether you planned this alone…or if Mystify was in on it with you."

*You continue to surprise me, Ava,* Adrianna said with what sounded and felt like genuine amazement and appreciation.

"I-I-I…" Claude sputtered.

"It was you working with the Templars." I pointed a finger. "And it was you that had Prince Fraylee convinced that he needed to back out of the deal he made with them."

"That is preposterous," Claude spat, finally finding his voice. The problem was that he now sounded like a kid caught with his hand in the cookie jar.

"What was the deal that you and Mystify made?" I asked.

A groan distracted me and I turned to see the bugbears had placed themselves around Morgan. Only, they didn't look so confident. I am not professing to be an expert on reading the expressions of giant, furry looking creatures that resemble the post-midnight feeding version of a mogwai, but the droopy ears and the lack of a snarl on their lips was telling.

Also, I noticed that the revenants had moved back to the arch of the entry hall. They were watching me closely, and their open cowering told me all that I needed to now.

"Get away from her," I growled to the bugbears.

I could resume my little confrontation with Claude in a moment, but something told me that I needed to take care of Morgan...that she was some sort of priority. I thought that strange since we had not been seeing eye-to-eye lately...or ever.

I was almost surprised when the three beasts did as I told them. They took several steps back and now joined the revenants in the arch. I hurried over and took my place above the visibly broken and damaged Psychic. Looking at her made me hurt, but the funny thing was that I still could not smell her. I could pick out the giant, the revenants. But I was also getting something new; Gordon, and...

"Race!" I blurted.

The man had pulled himself up to a sitting position. His skin was an angry red and covered in blisters, the one on his cheek now almost the size of a golf ball and looking like it would burst any moment. Blood ran down from a cut on his forehead and made him look...sexy?

*What the hell is wrong with you, Ava?*

No, that was not Adrianna's voice in my head, it was my own. And honestly, I had to agree. This room was a scene of carnage on a massive level, Morgan was little more than a pulpy mess, Race looked like he had just stepped out of a blast furnace, a giant had been decapitated and gushed a small lake's worth of blood onto the stone floor and, from the smell of it, I had my doubts as to whether Gordon had survived his injuries.

"I need you to focus, ghoul," a voice cut through my senses. My head snapped up to discover Blodwen standing beside me and looking down at Morgan with just a hint of concern on her crone face.

"Enough already," I turned my head and fixed her with my black eyes, "you know my name. Try using it."

"I am not here at your pleasure...nor are we friends," the voice replied with its flat, evil sounding tone.

Seriously, what was her deal? Her other form was so much more appealing. Why did she even bother with this one? And the voices…this one had a bit of a hiss to it and just did not sound human. It did not even fit the old crone face that it came from. But when she was in her Venus form, she was just…

Well she wasn't unpleasant, let's just leave it at that.

"She is here as *my* guest," Claude laughed. "And since I have invited her in and shown hospitality, she is bound by honor not to do me any harm."

Oh yeah…I had almost forgotten about Claude.

I turned to the bugbears and gave them what I hoped was my most menacing stare. "Secure him," I growled.

The bugbears looked at one another, and I could see their big pointy, tufted ears twitching. I had to wonder if that was some form of non-verbal communication. At last, one of them looked at me and bared his teeth.

"We sense your power and must obey," it said in a growly voice that sounded like somebody had trained a Pit Bull to talk.

The three bugbears sprang before Claude could do a thing. I had no idea where the gold cord came from that they tied him up with, and I only briefly wondered if it might have some sort of magic power. While this went on, I kept my eyes on the revenants. They had retreated into the darkest shadows, and all that remained to be seen if you were just using the naked eye would have been three sets of red, glowing orbs. Of course I could see them just fine, and I was glad that they made no moves towards me or the bugbears.

"You are here at my pleasure…I welcomed you in and showed you hospitality!" Claude screamed at Blodwen.

I had no idea what that had to do with anything, but then I still did not know what a gwyll was and how they differed from a regular faerie.

"That does not mean that I have to help you in any way," Blodwen said, turning to face the angry, sputtering Psychic. "You have been untruthful to me and led me to believe that you had things in order. You assured me that the faerie were protected and that this female ghoul would be dispatched."

112

"Why are you so intent on me being killed?" I blurted. "Just because we aren't pals does not mean that you need to have me killed."

"You are a female ghoul…and thus, you cannot be allowed to live. It is simply too much of a danger to my kind. And now that I have seen you…in action," she glanced at the sprawled corpse of the jötunn, "I am more certain than ever that you are a threat that must be put down. I curse myself for not killing you when I had the chance."

"But—" I tried to protest.

*If you are going to save Morgan, you need to get her home*, Adrianna said, cutting me off.

*What about Race…I think Gordon might be dead…and Claude? I can't just…leave*, I could hear myself whining even in my own head. It wasn't pretty.

*Morgan is going to die if you do not get her home right now*, Adrianna said. It was not said with passion or anything resembling concern. She was simply stating a fact.

*How am I going to get her home?* I asked.

I could feel Adrianna pause. There was something really big coming, and I was not going to like it one bit. Of that I had no doubt.

She explained and I tried not to cringe. I even heard Cody whistle in the background. I had almost forgotten that he was here. When she told me what I had to do, I almost felt sick.

*And you are sure about this?* I asked.

*I am sure that Morgan's only chance resides with you*, Adrianna replied.

I turned to Blodwen who was eyeing me with disdain. I was not proud of myself or what I was about to do. I saw that look in her eyes change as she obviously saw something in my face that set off her internal alarms.

With a thought, I willed my claws into being and advanced.

Next, on a Very Special *That Ghoul Ava...*

# 13

## Bad Girls

"Just as I suspected!" Blodwen accused. She had returned to her Venus form. Maybe she knew that I found that more appealing, and thus, perhaps I would be dissuaded from my course of action.

Nope.

Her hands made a rolling motion and I saw that blue ball of icy electric power start to form. I had a feeling that this was going to sting; and not just physically. In the past twenty-four hours, I had become a killer. I could make any excuse I wanted about the necessity of the situation. I could even brush aside the fact that I'd merely killed goblins in order to further a theory about the zombie.

No matter how you try to justify it, murder is murder. When you set out to kill something or someone, you are making a choice. In that instant, unless it is an act of defense or mercy, then you are the bad guy. There is no way to dress it up and make it pretty.

"If it makes a difference, I am terribly sorry," I said.

"Ava!" I heard Race protest. He had managed, through some miracle, to climb to his feet. "Ava, by the Order of the Templar, I command you to stop!"

"I don't fall under your jurisdiction, Race," I said, my eyes not leaving Blodwen.

"If you do this, you will be registered as a lethal monster under the laws of the Templar. I will have no choice but to come after you," Race said in a voice that sounded strangely like he was pleading with me. That was weird. I thought that the Templars wanted to exterminate ghouls. Why would this make things any worse?

"Ava," a voice that nobody would have heard if not for the super senses that a ghoul possesses, spoke. Now, I have no idea of the auditory perception abilities of bugbears, revenants, Templars, or Gwyllion, but I heard it as clear as if she were speaking in my ear.

"Morgan?" I looked down at the mess at my feet.

"Do not go down that path. If you do, there will be no turning back," Morgan said.

I wanted to scream. She was talking in that same emotionless voice that she always used. She might as well be telling me I am an idiot or giving me my next job.

"But you will die," I insisted. "This is the only chance to save you."

My eyes flicked back up to Blodwen. Her beautiful face was made even more so as her wide eyes fixed on my razor fingers and her mouth open in an "oh" of fear.

"I have lived a long life, and I came here knowing very well what might happen. The closer I got, the more that dark sense of impending death became, but I had to come. You had to know."

"Know what?" I felt my blood run cold. Okay, we have gone over this before; I know that I am technically dead and my blood is already room temperature at the very best...but you get the point.

"Lisa has been taken...Belinda has disappeared."

At first, it was just a bunch of random words. It made no sense to me and refused to sink in. Then my mind began to whirl. Was she saying that Belinda had taken Lisa? Were the two events linked, or were they each a separate problem?

"A new vampire has arrived in my district...and there has been a series of deaths among the Supernatural community."

I was still trying to make sense of everything when a ball of energy hit me square in the chest. In turning my attention to Morgan, I had entirely forgotten about Blodwen. I'd made an advance towards her and then stopped. She had done what any smart creature faced with its possible demise would do—she let me have it.

"You should have taken the time while I was distracted to simply run away," I snarled. Now I was angry and my mind was coming up with all sorts of reasons why I was now well within my rights to eat the hag.

I took two steps, covering half the distance between me and my target. Raising my switch-fingered hands, I prepared to literally cut her in half.

*Hurry!* Adrianna encouraged. *Can't you feel it?*

It was like a switch being turned on. Unlike my ghoulish sense that could always detect death, this was almost like an alarm. Never before had I been able to get anything from any of my senses when it came to Morgan, but all of a sudden, there was this feeling coursing through me.

*What the hell?* I asked, making sure to keep it inside as I advanced on the now cowering Blodwen, ready to take those last two steps into something that would forever taint my soul.

*You are sensing a very powerful being that is near death. If you were to enact the ritual, you could create...*

*A powerful zombie*, I finished for her.

I brought my claws down and was stunned when they came to a sudden stop. When had Race crossed the room to me?

"Don't do this, Ava," he warned with even more urgency. "This is not who you are. Lisa has spent weeks trying to convince anybody who would listen that you are not like the ghouls of old. She has insisted that you are actually a good...*person*."

"That is where she was wrong," I replied flatly, feeling the emotion slip from me. *Oh, God, please don't let me say the words that are swirling on the tip of my tongue*, I thought. Then...I said them.

"I am a monster...I stopped being a person a long time ago. I have been trying to be the same as I was before...this!" I ran my hands down the length of my body to indicate myself. "And that has been my problem. I keep hearing everybody tell me just what a ghoul can do…how they were feared and considered so powerful that an attempt was made to wipe them…*us*…out completely. And I ignored all of that as I let everybody sort of walk on me. Funny…but that was exactly what I did as a human, and where did that lead? A bottle of White Zin and some pills in a bathroom. Why was I so surprised when nobody noticed?"

*You have to act now, Ava,* Adrianna warned. *You have the choice before you. Do what I suggested…or allow Morgan to die.*

"I'm sorry," I whispered.

Race braced himself, but I could see that he was barely able to stand. That jötunn had hurt him far worse than he was letting on. With a sweep of my feet, I took his out from under him. He landed with a pained grunt and I moved past him to Blodwen.

The gwyll stood cowering, her eyes not able to leave my long-nailed fingers. I refused to close my eyes as I swiped across the old hag's midsection. Sure enough, her upper body fell one way and her lower the other.

I plunged my left hand's switch-fingers into the upper body and opened wide. The sensation was beyond anything that I'd ever felt. It was even more amazing than when I had peeled off bits of Adrianna's dead skin that night in the graveyard and eaten it like potato chips.

This was the equivalent to a ghoul's energy drink. My remaining injuries mended instantly and completely and the cold burn on my chest vanished. I grabbed the lower half and wolfed it down in seconds.

My eyes felt it first…there was a tingle that felt almost like somebody had touched them after charging up with static electricity.

*Nooooo!* a voice wailed in my head. *Please forgive me, my kindred!* It was Blodwen, and she was in my mind.

I did not even have to try. My eyes instantly found the doorway that Adrianna insured would be there. I picked up Morgan's limp form.

*Oh my goodness*, I said inwardly. I could smell Morgan! She was like refreshingly sweet and tangy citrus mixed with…flowers? That was kind of weird, but I didn't have time to ponder it. I headed for the doorway that I was now certain only I could see.

"What shall we do with…this?" one of the bugbears called, shaking Claude's bound figure.

"Whatever you like," I said, all emotion gone.

As I stepped through the doorway, I could hear Race hurling threats at me. *"The Templars would have no choice…blah-blah-blah."* Yes, well I didn't have a choice either.

I fixed my thoughts on Morgan and home. I sensed Adrianna's approval along with Blodwen's horror. I had entered a way-gate. It was an ancient method of travel for the faerie. Used properly, I could practically travel anyplace. It did have its limits. I could not travel from one continent to the next. The oceans were massive roadblocks.

There was a blurring flash of blue and green that reminded me of when the *Millennium Falcon* would go into hyperspace. It all happened in a matter of a heartbeat; I was actually doing nothing more than completing my initial step—the same one that I had taken as I entered the doorway. However, now I was stepping out of the doorway. I felt my skin tingle all over with a cooling sensation, and suddenly, I was in a huge, dark room with furniture that looked like it came from a museum.

I felt something cold slide over my skin and looked around in panic. I had no idea where I had stepped out. I was relieved to see that I was not rimmed in fire like I had that first time that I had ventured down into the sidhe after my battle with Prince Fraylee and Merriette. I think that I was even more relieved to see that Morgan was not rimmed in fire or anything.

*Set her down on that couch*, Adrianna said in a rushed tone that surprised me. Since when did she care at all about my Psychic…or anybody? Still, I did as she instructed. She had been very helpful up to this point.

Without warning, the door behind me slammed open. I spun, claws at the ready and fully prepared to do battle. Or at least that was the case until I saw who was standing in the doorway.

"Ava!" Lisa cried, rushing towards me, but then stopping short when she saw the ruined lump that was Morgan. "What have you done?" Her voice had changed to one of wariness and she skidded to a halt.

"What?" I glanced over my shoulder and realized with sudden dread just how this might look.

I was standing over the body with a murder weapon in my hands…or hands that could easily be murder weapons. It was made worse by the fact that they were still dripping with all manner of blood from the events back at Claude's.

"Move aside, child," a voice spoke from the entry. Betty entered the room and regarded me with nothing more than a raised eyebrow.

The elderly woman (or whatever she was) stepped into the room. For some reason, I took a step back and put myself between her and Morgan. So much had happened in the past few hours, and I simply had no trust to give anybody. My eyes shot past Betty and fixed on Lisa. Okay…let me amend that earlier statement. I could trust *one* person.

"Don't come any closer," I snarled.

"Ava, you can't help her any more than you have," Betty said calmly. "Honestly…I am more than a little surprised to see you here. I have no idea how you managed it."

"Is it safe?" another voice called from what I now had to assume was either a hallway or a damned packed auditorium. Seriously…where did all these people come from and how did they know to be here where I had stepped through?

"How is she here?" Rain asked as she shoved through whatever was gathered outside that door. As I took another look around, I realized that it was the only door out of this lavishly furnished room.

Blodwen whimpered in my head, but before I could do anything, Adrianna snarled some sort of warning in a language that I did not understand. However…the menace and threat came across clearly.

"We can worry about that later," Betty said as she closed the distance between us.

Before I could react, she had shot past me and was kneeling beside Morgan who was making no sound as she lie there in a bloody mess. For some reason, my mind went to the idea that she was ruining what I knew had to be a very expensive couch.

"I did not do this," I said, finally finding my voice.

"Of course you didn't," Betty said absently as she huddled over Morgan.

"What happened?" Lisa gasped. I heard the relief in her voice and I was certain that it came from Betty's assurance that I had nothing to do with Morgan's injuries. Still, it hurt to know that she thought me capable.

I quickly related as much as I could. I kept my narrative to just Morgan and her arrival. I had to include the fight with the giant, but as for the Templars, Blodwen, and even of all the events that took place down in that basement prison, I remained silent.

When I finished, I knew right away that Lisa could see through my omissions. I was not ready to call them lies; I hadn't mentioned a great many things nor made any sort of denials.

"I want to know how she comes to be here!" Rain demanded, and I felt a new sheet of cold wash over me.

*Uh-oh,* I thought.

Next, on a Very Special *That Ghoul Ava...*

# 14

## That Was Then, This Is Now

"I thought she was a friend," Lisa was sputtering. "And she has been here before...so what is the big deal?"

*Hmm...big surprise.* Ava is lost again. I had no clue what they were talking about.

"She is in the HEART of the sidhe! Nobody comes in here but for the Godmother and invited guests," Rain said with what really sounded like a building head of angry steam.

*They will discover you now, ghoul!* Blodwen screamed from somewhere deep and distant in my mind.

*How is that possible?* I was not even done with that thought when the realization struck. This had to do with some residual power I had gained from eating Blodwen. That meant—

*You can travel the sidhe at will,* Adrianna said with cold certainty. *And it has sealed your fate!*

"Friend or not," Rain said with an authority that I had never witnessed from the girl before, "she has invaded the sanctity of the sidhe. This is our home...the one place where we can be confident of our safety. Her appearance here removes that certainty. It can only mean one thing."

"What is that?" Lisa asked, the dread in her voice just as clear on her face.

"That she has the fabled ability of a female ghoul...and that

123

she has killed a Godmother of ancient blood. That is the only way that she could enter our home without the defenses turning their full fury on her...and the one she carried here."

*All too easy*, Adrianna's voice was now more what I was used to as it dripped with evil glee. I felt an uneasy feeling course through me along with the worst case of "buyer's remorse" imaginable. I had bought into Adrianna's ploy...bit the worm and bought it hook, line, and sinker.

"What did you do, Ava?" Lisa whispered.

"Everybody hush!" Betty snapped. "Right now I need to focus all my energy on Morgan, and I can't do it with you all clucking like wet hens!"

*Fine with me*, I thought. I was not looking forward to answering any of the onslaught of questions that were sure to come fast and furious. Also, that gave me the opportunity to turn my thoughts inward.

*What have you done?* I thundered in my head. I heard Cody squeak and then I actually felt his presence shrink as if he were trying to hide. Blodwen remained constant, but she was almost ignoring me. As for Adrianna, she was standing her ground.

*I have done nothing but help you realize your potential*, the former self-proclaimed Queen of the Zombies replied coolly.

*Why don't I believe you?* I glanced over at Lisa and could see her seeming to almost dissect me with her eyes. I did not like the degree of scrutiny I was receiving from her.

To add to my discomfort, Rain was now in a cluster with a handful of other faeries. The girls were huddled close, and a head would pop up on occasion to glare at me or cast a look that you would expect to see from a zebra at a watering hole where tigers were known to frequent. They were not only scared and visibly upset, but they were angry. I wondered briefly why I could not hear them with my ghoul super-hearing.

The faeries I could dismiss, but when it came to Lisa, I was hoping beyond hope that I would be able to plead my case to her. Not just the situation I currently found myself in, but also how we had parted that last time in my room where I had tried my very hardest to see how much of my foot I could shove in my mouth.

"Ava," Betty called, breaking me out of my attempt to get a pity party started. I turned and went over to where the woman hunched above Morgan's unmoving and very messy figure. God help me, she smelled delicious.

I stared down at a lump that I only knew to be Morgan because I had laid her there. She was so broken and mangled that I honestly did not understand what force of nature kept her alive. I also could not help but wonder if it might be best to hurry and end her suffering.

"Ava," a voice came up from that mess.

There was an instant silence in the room. While I had not been able to actually hear the faeries or, at the very least, make out what they were saying, it was obvious that they had contributed to the ambient noise of the room. If I thought that it had been kind of quiet before, there was now an almost complete absence of sound. It seemed that the entire universe had suddenly gone silent to hear what I was sure had to be the final words of this Psychic.

"Ava, please forgive me," Morgan managed in a wet rasp. "I was foolish."

There was no situation that I could imagine where those words would come out of Morgan's mouth. Not that I had not thought them or something to that effect at some time, but I sure never believed that she would utter them.

"Should you be wasting energy talking?" I asked lamely.

"I should have brought you in, but I was foolish. I did not believe that your presence would be discovered so quickly. Even worse, I refused to believe the old accounts of the powers of a female ghoul. It seemed so impossible..." Morgan let out a sigh and there was a long moment of silence where I was certain that she was dead. At last, she continued, "You are not supposed to be possible. The Templars failed to eliminate all of the ghouls...but the female line was supposed to have been severed. Yet...here you are."

"I don't understand," I managed.

I felt a lump growing in my throat. If you would have asked

me at any time prior to this very moment if I cared whether Morgan lived or died, I would have easily said that I did not. Funny thing about that, it is easy to say anything if you do not believe that you will ever face that event or action.

"Yes...I know you don't understand, Ava...and that is my fault. I should have treated you like what the legends suggested. And now I have lost you."

She was being silly. Well...unless she meant that she was about to die, in which case, I could definitely see her point.

"You have not lost me," I decided to speak the obvious since it was a possibility that she might actually survive. "I am right here. I brought you back and I am not going anywhere."

"But you do not have a choice," Morgan said around a mouthful of blood. I glanced at Betty who was kneeling beside me with her eyes shut. Her lips were moving in what had to be either a spell or prayer. "You consumed Mystify. Betty and I miscalculated—"

There was a small cough and I noticed that Betty's eyes had opened. She glanced up at me and then closed them again, returning to whatever it was that she was doing.

"Okay...*I* miscalculated. Betty warned me from the start that you were showing all of the signs. It just seemed so...unlikely."

"You need to tell me what is going on," I almost cried. I could hear my voice crack just a little. "I am so lost...so confused."

"A female ghoul absorbs the powers of any Supernatural that she consumes. A male does as well, but only for a limited period." Betty made a pass with her hands over Morgan and there was a green glow that covered her for just a moment and then seemed to be absorbed into Morgan's body. "Your consumption of Mystify has had some unforeseen...consequences."

I glanced over at Rain and her little group. They were now all looking at me like I was a complete stranger. I had slammed the doors on Adrianna, Blodwen and even Cody—although he had been as quiet as a church mouse from almost the very beginning—to keep their voices out of my head for the time being.

I needed to concentrate on what was being said to me.

"And when we had you consume Adrianna, it was really just a test. Only, nothing seemed to happen, so we assumed that the ancient stories were false." Betty stood and faced me. "We were wrong…and I apologize."

"Then she has committed the act we were warned of…and thus can come unbidden and unwelcome to any sidhe that she wishes?" Rain gasped.

"Wait!" I threw my hands up to quiet the murmurs and even a few wails and shrieks of horror that came from the group of clustered faeries. "You guys were just in my house the other day…snaking on pomegranates and acting like it was no big deal. All of a sudden you think something has changed? I am still the same person that you met…I am not some scary monster or boogeyman."

"Yet here you stand…in the very heart of the sidhe. You entered via our private gate, and the sidhe does not defend itself as it would against any who come without explicit invitation." Rain stepped forward from the group and drew her shoulders up in an expression of confident authority.

Rain was suddenly a very different woman from what I remembered. When we'd met, she was nothing more than a silly girl. I was actually a bit surprised when I found out that she had become Godmother after the death of Merriette.

"I know I probably have some explaining to do, but I hope that you will give me a chance before declaring me as Public Enemy Number One. I only did what I had been advised to do when I sought to save Morgan. Adrianna was being very helpful—" I was explaining in a bit of a rush.

"The Queen of the Zombies?" one of the faerie girls behind Rain gasped.

"So she is still within you?" Betty asked. Morgan stirred a bit, but she only managed a soft moan, so I was not exactly sure if she was reacting to her pain or my admission.

"Umm…yeah," I answered. I thought that was a given.

Betty took a step back and I saw Lisa grimace. What did they know that I did not?

"And you say that she has *guided* you...been helpful?" Betty asked with what sounded like a mix of caution and skepticism.

"Ava?" Lisa stepped up to me and looked me in the eyes. But it was not like she was actually looking *at* me, more like she was trying to peer inside my eyes and see if I was there.

"What?" I folded my arms over my stomach and scowled. I didn't like being looked at like I was some sort of window display.

"How do we tell?" Lisa asked over my shoulder like I was not standing right there.

"Tell what?" I asked, making no attempt to hide my growing annoyance.

"It is her," Morgan's voice came in a choked rasp. "I feel certain that she would have made no attempt to bring me here if Adrianna had wrested control."

"Excuse me?" I blurted.

"I want her to make a vow here in the heart of the sidhe," Rain demanded. "If it is really Ava, then she will do so, and we can be done with all of this."

"I need everybody to just settle down. This is too much for me!" I was almost ready to cry. I had not been this frustrated since my high school final in physics. Oh...and I got a 'D' in case you really wanted to know.

"Yep, that's Ava," Lisa said with a shrug.

"Can you feel Adrianna in you now?" Betty moved up and stood beside Lisa; she too was peering into my eyes like she was trying to see something on the other side of a window.

"I have her locked up, but she's here," I admitted. "Also, Cody is in here...he is some kind of necromancer that Mystify had locked up in his dungeon trying to create zombies...and did you know that brains are some sort of recharging food for them? How crazy is that?" I was suddenly babbling, almost unable to quit talking.

"Yes, I think we can be sure that it is her," Morgan coughed.

"I want her to make a vow!" Rain repeated, sounding like a child on the verge of a tantrum.

"Maybe you need to stop telling me what to do," I snapped. "I won't be making any vows or promises until I know what the heck is going on, so you and your little faerie friends can just sit down, shut up, and wait your turn. When I know what is going on…then we can talk about promises." I looked over Betty's shoulder to where Morgan was still in a lumpy mess on the couch. "And can I at least assume that she is going to be okay?"

"Morgan will be fine," Betty assured me. "She is here in the heart of the sidhe…it is mending her, but that will take some time. And now, can I ask how you knew to bring her here to be healed?"

"I told you…Adrianna told me. Of course I had to…" I glanced at Rain, "…I had to do something first, and I think that might be why the faeries are so upset."

"Oh…I am certain of that," Betty agreed.

I could feel Adrianna suddenly struggling to get free from her isolation. I doubled my efforts and was surprised when her resistance ceased immediately.

"So…" I clapped my hands together, "how much trouble am I in with everybody?"

Lisa paled, but before she could speak, Rain spoke, "You will make the vow, and you will do so now, or we will consider you an enemy of not only the whole of the faerie realm, but of the sidhe as well."

*Somebody was awfully full of herself*, I thought.

"She will do nothing until Morgan has absorbed all of her healing and is able to depart of her own will," Betty argued.

"*Morgan* is not my concern," Rain shot back. I didn't know if she was aware enough to hear this, but I have to admit that I took just a teensy bit of pleasure in hearing somebody else spoken of as if they were something to be wiped from the bottom of a shoe. "We are not under her jurisdiction. The faerie do not answer—"

"Stop it!" I barked, stepping between the pair who had been taking one agonizingly slow step towards each other after another as each spoke. "I won't make any vows until I am damn good and ready. You want to call me an enemy, go ahead. You won't be alone. And I got news for you," I put one finger right in Rain's face after I quickly made sure that none of my digits were sporting long blades, "you don't want to piss me off right now. I have had a very bad day, but I am starting to figure out why the old legends about ghouls were so terrifying. And if I can get my powers under control, you have every reason to fear me. But here is the funny thing…I have done nothing to deserve this treatment."

"You are a ghoul…the unholy," Rain said in a tight whisper.

I was now looking her in the eye. What I saw did not resemble anything that I had seen from her before. Instead, I saw the same look that I'd seen from Blodwen.

"I don't know where this whole thing about me being unholy came from," I sputtered, the anger making it difficult for me to get my words out in a tone and at a volume that did not chip steel or melt glass, "but I am still Ava Birch. Yes…I am a ghoul now, and yes, that makes me a bit different from the waitress I used to be, but dammit…I am still Ava!"

"You are an abomination!" Rain shrieked. "You have consumed one of ours…you killed Prince Fraylee, the last male of the oldest blood line in our history…and now perhaps we must consider that you did so with other motives."

"You know what—" I lunged, my fingers unleashing their blades before I even knew it. Lisa jumped in front of me and put herself between me and the Godmother.

"Ava!" the young girl yelled in my face. My eyes flicked to her and I felt my rage almost evaporate.

All of my worry and concern about where we stood, Lisa and I, or if there was any chance that our friendship would be able to exist…it all vanished in seconds. She was looking at me with all of the care, love, and compassion that I could take.

Lisa Jenkins might wear a Templar ring, she might do things that I don't know about, but she was still my friend…my best friend in the entire world. And if you have never looked into somebody's eyes and seen that absolute acceptance—that look that assures you that, no matter what you do in life, you will have one person who will still be there at your side—well then, you have my pity.

"This is our home…this is our sidhe," Rain said, bringing my attention back to the situation at hand. "I demand that you depart."

"You will demand nothing!" Betty pushed past me and Lisa. I don't know who was more surprised; me, Lisa, or Rain. "Ava Birch is a ghoul, that much is true. She has been out on a limb by herself for these past several months with almost no guidance. However, it is now clear that the ancient texts that tell of the powers possessed by the female ghouls are not just an exaggerated bunch of legends. The stories are true. Are you prepared to have a ghoul as an enemy, Godmother?"

Whoa! Betty had just pulled out the Godmother card! A stirring caused me to glance over to where Morgan was struggling to get up to a sitting position. Even through the mask of blood that covered her face, I could see interest etched clearly on it.

"The ghouls almost wiped out every breed of faerie…the female known as Boudicca went on a rampage through every sidhe," Rain wept. "The death…the near utter destruction…"

No wonder the faeries hated ghouls and wanted them all dead. If I was hearing Rain correctly, we had almost destroyed them first.

"That was then, this is now." I stepped over and took Rain's hands in mine. Yes, I did notice her flinch, but I was going to write that off to her reaction to quoting one of the lesser known songs by The Monkees. "I can't do anything about what was done before, but I am not like that…I can't do or say anything that makes all of the terrible events of the past just go away, but I can promise you that I am different."

A silence fell and I looked around. Lisa had a confused look on her face that reflected how I felt. Betty was looking around like she was expecting horrible beasts to erupt from the shadows and Rain had her head tilted, a look of calm making her look even more beautiful than she already was had smoothed away the anger.

Next, on a Very Special *That Ghoul Ava...*

# 15

## Promises, Promises

"She speaks truth," one of the faeries gasped.

"That's interesting," Betty and Morgan said in near perfect unison.

"What?" I looked around the room and could not help but notice the massive change in everybody—with the exception of me and Lisa, we both remained clueless. "What is so interesting?"

"You spoke words and made a promise that you could not possibly hope to control," Morgan managed from the couch. I swear that she was getting stronger by the second.

"Umm…huh?" I know. Not very articulate, but that was the best I had at this point.

"You made a promise within the confines of the Heart of the Sidhe," Rain said. She stepped up to me and ran her hand down the length of my arm and then reached up to caress my face. She was very gentle, and if I was being honest, it was not only very sexy, but it was pushing my buttons.

"Okay!" I raised my hands, being as gentle-but-firm as I could in pushing Rain's hand away. I took a step back and shot a raised eyebrow look of question at Betty.

"A promise given in the sidhe is binding…it has power," Betty explained.

"You made a statement about your nature, though," Morgan said, rising to her feet in an unsteady lurch. "It would be like somebody saying that they are a good person. Okay…compared to what? If you compared yourself to Pol Pot, Josef Stalin, or Maximilien Robespierre, it would be easy to make such a claim."

Okay, I was starting to get what she was saying, but I was torn between being utterly clueless as to who the hell Maximilien Robs-a-diddly was and the fact that Morgan was explaining something. I was afraid to ask a follow up, so I simply nodded and listened.

"Yet, you made a statement that you are somehow different from the female ghoul of the past. The first problem would be that you have no idea what sort of baseline you would be judged against. However, the sidhe would know…the sidhe is sentient, it has a memory. It would seem that, at least for the moment, the sidhe concurs with your statement."

Morgan stepped before me, gently nudging Rain aside, and placed a hand on my shoulder. While I was still amazed over how anything that looked as battered as she did could move, much less walk or talk, I was also quick to realize that I could no longer smell her.

"If you have said this without any sort of reprisal from the sidhe, then…" Morgan's voice trailed off and she stepped back.

"Then it is truth," Rain finished the statement. "While it would not be able to kill her outright, the sidhe would be able to reduce her to something that we could box up and dispose of if her words were false."

"You are more than you seem, Ava Birch," Morgan said with a bow. "And I owe you my life. I would have died if you had not acted."

"Umm…yeah," I said with a slow drawl. "But that is where things get sort of wonky again." Everybody was looking at me like I was the most interesting thing in the world. I was not entirely comfortable with that sort of attention. "Adrianna is the one who guided me."

"She would have known the healing power that resides in

the Heart of the Sidhe. It is something of legend, and a very powerful magic that can bring back any being from the brink of death. It cannot reverse the process, but as long as any residue of life remains, the Heart of the Sidhe can heal." Betty sounded like a schoolmarm as she dropped information on me.

"Why would Adrianna want to heal Morgan?" Lisa blurted. Good for her in asking the very question that was on the tip of my tongue. And I had not forgotten that Miss Lisa Jenkins was supposed to be missing or in Italy. I was going to ask her about that…someday…maybe.

"I do not believe that was her ultimate goal. I believe that she did what she always does, which is use any tool at her disposal to reach her end means. In this case, I believe she had something rather insidious in mind."

"Okay…I'll bite, what do you think she had planned?" I said, once more making certain that all the current occupants of my mind were secure and unable to intrude. Oh yeah, I paid special attention to Adrianna. Once more, The Queen of the Zombies had proved to be a threat.

"She had to know that the faeries would not be happy that you had managed to enter their sidhe. Bringing you here to the Heart would be the most grievous affront possible. Even a creature as powerful as a ghoul would not be able to stand against the full fury of a Godmother who tapped into the power of the Heart.

"If you were brought down, you would be weak. During that time, I am certain that Adrianna would have made an attempt to wrest control of your being."

Betty was dumping a lot of knowledge on me, but the funny thing was that it was making sense! And that made me think back on something from earlier.

"What is a Mindwalk?" I asked.

"Dear goddess of mercy!" Morgan gasped. Betty just made a slight snort.

"Is it bad?" I looked around at the two. I shot a look at Rain, but she seemed lost. Okay, this was not something that the faeries were up to speed on.

"It is..." Morgan started, and I swear that her voice had reverted almost completely to her prior, unemotional self, "...dangerous. How have you come across such knowledge?"

Now it was my turn. I had a choice here of telling her what I knew—although I had to admit that it was not very much—or I could take a shot at being secretive. I decided that the latter would probably not do me any favors, plus I was not sure if a lie or some sort of deception would turn the Heart of the Sidhe against me.

I decided that, if I was as sick of all the secrets as I had been saying, that now was a good time to be on the level. I told them in as much detail as I could about what had happened at Claude's. I told about Gretch, about Cody and his Fembots. All the while, I was relating everything that transpired between Adrianna and me during the entire ordeal. I was surprised that I did not get interrupted by a gazillion questions when I told about my little "Alice Down the Rabbit Hole" experience.

I finished with my arrival here at the Heart of the Sidhe. I had made it a point to avoid Rain's gaze when I got to the part about killing and eating Blodwen. However, now that I was finished, I took a deep breath and looked her in the eyes.

"If you hate me and never want me to return, I understand," I said. And I meant it...Heart of the Sidhe or not.

"You devoured Blodwen Cadwallader, Queen of the Celtic Mulingar Gwyllion, Holder of the Blue Sphere, and Cosantóir of the Ten Sidhe?" Rain gasped.

I gasped also, but it was mostly due to the fact that she let that title roll off her tongue so effortlessly. Seriously, I felt good about myself if I could name my state's governor, the President of the United States, and the last guy that I slept with.

"Umm...yes?"

"A Gwyllion? You consumed a Gwyllion?" Rain pressed.

"I guess." I still did not actually know what a Gwyllion was, but she had seemed pretty sure of herself, and I had to think that she was rather important.

Rain turned to her gaggle of faeries girlfriends and they all began to twitter in what I had to assume was their native language. It was really high-pitched, and I wondered how many dogs in the area were perking up and wondering what the hell was going on. Betty and Morgan kept silent. I didn't know if it was because they were listening in or what, but they kept looking back and forth to each other and then to me. I was almost certain that I was in big trouble.

At last, Rain turned back to me. Stepping away from her flock, she smoothed an imaginary wrinkle from her sleeve and then held her head up as straight as possible like she was trying to add an extra inch or two to her height.

"It is decided," she announced.

*Swell*, I thought, *can we just get this over with?*

"You are forgiven under the condition that you vow to serve at my behest for the duration of one day that will be at my choosing."

One day? I tried not to smirk. I mean, what was she gonna have me do? Take out the trash? Do a "Wormy Dog" around the room?

Please don't tell me you do not know what a "Wormy Dog" is! Okay...actually, I learned this one at camp. The way it works is that you sit down, plant your hands between your slightly spread legs and scoot on your butt using your heels and the palms of your hands to propel you around the room—or down the middle of the cabin—yelping doggy noises are usually optional. It is fairly embarrassing, but nothing that I couldn't handle.

"Sure," I said with a shrug.

Of course I said that almost at the exact same time that Morgan and Betty yelled, "NO!" I looked at the pair and saw what appeared to be actual concern.

"You need to vow it before the Heart of the Sidhe," Rain said after she gave a glare at the two women who were obviously against this idea. Personally, I did not see the problem.

"Ava!" Morgan hissed, her voice thick with warning and...was that concern? I think I was touched.

"It is just one day," I said. "What's the big deal?"

"You will be completely at her command," Morgan replied,

her lips pressed so tight that I was amazed that words could actually escape them.

"Umm…maybe she has a point," Lisa offered.

"What if she commands you to kill Miss Jenkins?" Morgan pressed. "You would be bound to do as you are bid. And if you make the vow, the sidhe can compel you."

"Even if I didn't want to?" I asked. I know…pretty stupid question, but I had a hard time seeing Rain as the sort who would have me do something…evil.

"I vow that I will not send you after Lisa Jenkins," Rain said. She stepped forth and took my hands. "Ava, this could be the start of something new and wonderful. You must trust me. Make the vow."

"I vow to this agreement thingy," I said.

Nothing.

I guess I was expecting a chime or a flash of light. But honestly, nothing happened. In my head I could hear Marvin the Martian saying, *"Where was the ka-boom? There was supposed to be an earth-shattering ka-boom!"*

Maybe I didn't say it right. That thought vanished the moment that I saw Rain's expression. She was smiling…kind of like the cat that just ate the canary. Hmm…would that make me…Tweety Bird?

"So when does this start?" I finally asked after a silence that was way too long and far too uncomfortable.

"I will call you, Ava," Rain answered. "Until that time, I will ask for you and the rest of your guests to depart. There is business to attend and it is clear that Morgan is now able to move on her own accord."

"Sure—" I barely had the word out of my mouth when there was a swirl of light and a feeling in my stomach like when I rode in an express elevator.

I looked around as everything sort of fizzled into existence around me. I was more than a little surprised to find myself in my house.

"Oh!" a voice squeaked in surprise. Aoife leapt to her feet and hurried over to me.

I was in my bedroom. Hmm…and so was Aoife? I could worry about that later, but right now, I needed to square a few things away.

"I need you to do me a favor," I said to the confused siren who was looking at me like I was a stranger.

"Yes, m-m-miss…" she sort of stammered as she took a step closer to me and tilted her head as if she might be studying me.

"Just keep an eye on me, and if things go bad, I need you to tell Morgan and Betty that I did a Mindwalk."

"A Mindwalk?" The confusion was clear in Aoife's voice.

"They will know what I am talking about," I said with a dismissive wave of my hand. Now how did I do that the last time?

Next, on a Very Special *That Ghoul Ava...*

# 16

## Church of the Poison Mind

I remembered something about *Alice in Wonderland* sort of being a part of things the last time. I focused my mind as much as I could and tried to figure out a way inside.

Nothing. I tried harder, and all that did was let the hounds loose so to speak. I could feel Adriana, Blodwen, and Cody with a much higher degree of clarity. The harder that I tried, the more of NOTHING that seemed to happen as I sought to Mindwalk.

*Interesting*, Adrianna mocked. *You have no idea what you did. It was nothing more than an accident. I should have known.*

A thought hit me and I clung to it. It was the thought of Adrianna. I could see her face, that sneer of derision etched on it. There was a soft pull, and then the spiral.

Ha! I all but shouted in triumph as I felt myself swirl and then stop. It was kind of dark…so I imagined brightness and, just like that, I was in a huge, gray, square room. All four walls were lined with doors. Three of those doors were wide open. I could see somebody standing in each one. In the first was Adrianna! My eyes flicked to a fourth door and I felt my lips press together and my nose wrinkle in distaste. The fourth door was scorched and completely covered with what appeared to be a bubbling, viscous tar-like substance.

I was only a little surprised to discover that Blodwen was in her Venus form. I had not even thought about it, but that alien sounding voice that I hated was gone. Now she was just that silky/sexy voice as well as her much more appealing guise. I would need to ask about that once I settled the important issues. And that reminded me…I glared at Adrianna.

"You lied…you set me up!" I snarled.

"I did what I had to do!" Adrianna retorted.

"Why did you have me kill Blodwen?" I was only just a little surprised when my fingers and toes went switchblade almost as quick as the idea of just thinking about it flashed across my mind.

"You need Morgan," Adrianna answered with her usual piss poor attitude. However, I did notice that she seemed to take a step back in retreat to the room or whatever it was on the other side of that door.

"You put me in the position of being Public Enemy Number One as far as the Templars are concerned."

"I got news for you, Ava…you already were. They will never allow a female ghoul to exist. You are a Weapon of Mass Destruction," Adrianna said as she faded further into the darkness beyond her doorway.

Blodwen made a sound that was one of agreement. The gwyll stepped toward me and was suddenly right before me. "On that I must agree. And perhaps there is a way that I can be of assistance. The way I see it, if you perish, then we are *all* gone for good." When she said the word "all", she shot a look over her shoulder towards Adrianna's door. "For better or worse, we reside in your mind chamber, and it is in all of our interests to see that you remain safe."

I looked around at the cavernous, empty chamber. I had a feeling that a lot of people would *not* be surprised to find so much empty space in my mind. Truthfully, it was disappointing. It was one thing for people to think you might be a bit of an airhead…quite another to confirm the rumor.

"But if the Templars are coming after me—" I began, but Blodwen cut me off.

"That was always the case, dear girl. They have been sworn

to that task, and it is simply a fact. Isn't there some sense of relief to have the mystery and wonder stripped away? Now you know it to be true."

"But I ate you!" I moaned. "Aren't you super pissed about that? I mean...well...I ate you! How could you be so calm now? I would totally hate me if I were you."

"And there is something to be said about that, but there is also something that you learn after living for centuries. You cannot bother yourself with things that you have absolutely no control over. My situation is what it is, and now I must make the best of it." Blodwen took my hands in hers. I felt a tingle and realized that my switchfingers and toes had retracted on their own at some point. "If you are different like you claim, perhaps the Supernatural world can become something greater. Perhaps it is *you* that will take us into the light...perhaps we will finally be able to come out from hiding."

"Whoa!" I pulled away. "I am not your girl. I was a freaking waitress...divorced...barely making it. I am not some sort of revolutionary."

"That is the human side of you still trying to infect your heart," Blodwen replied with a shake of her head.

I was so tired of hearing that "you're being a human" comment. I was who I was...or is it, I am who I am. Great...now I had Popeye the freaking sailorman's voice in my head.

"Whatever it is, it makes me certain that you have the wrong ghoul," I finally said.

"You can Mindwalk," Adrianna called from her doorway. "You should not be able to do that sort of thing. Like it or not, Ava Birch...you are special."

"Special or not, I came here for some answers and I have a feeling that one or both of you have at least some of them," I huffed.

"What about me?" Cody asked from his doorway. I let my gaze drift to him and was stunned to see him as a child of perhaps ten or twelve.

"I am pretty sure you have no answers for these questions," I said, giving my eyes a few hard blinks and a hard rubbing with the heel of my hands for good measure. I looked back at Blodwen. "Let's start with you guys. You are now back in that form of the attractive female, Cody looks like a kid, and Adrianna…" my voice trailed off as I turned to really give her a closer look.

She was still beautiful, had a stylish haircut, and the most hideous hands I had ever seen that were even worse than I remember if that is possible, but there were shadows flitting around her like tiny ghosts or something. Also, those comedy/tragedy masks on her legs had come out to look more like a sculpture. They were three-dimensional now…definitely not a tattoo. And yes, they were fully animated. The comedy mask even started leering at me like some sort of pervert.

"…Adrianna just looks like Adrianna always has," I finally said with a slight shrug of my shoulders.

"And this is how we shall remain," Blodwen said. "You have put us in these images because it is how you see us…or how your mind saw us perhaps is a better way of explaining it."

"Wait!" Cody blurted. "I'm some little kid in your eyes?"

"How do you see each other…yourselves?" I asked, ignoring the question.

"Exactly as you do." Blodwen glanced over at Cody, and a slight smile curved her lips up. Cody's door slammed shut with a bang.

"Okay…some answers." I looked over at Adrianna and waved her to come forward. "Let's start with that." My hand pointed to the door with all the dark, goopy stuff.

"Mystify has been sealed away," Adrianna said with a matter-of-factness that I found to be both refreshing and a little bit scary. She must have read something on my expression because she quickly continued. "He was a threat to you. All you need is his power."

"Okay, we can get back to that," I sighed. "Let's focus on *you*!" I pointed at Adrianna with an accusatory finger. "One minute I think you are helping me, the next I think you are trying to get me killed."

"Oh…make no mistake," Adrianna replied with all the menace she possessed coming through loud and clear in her voice. "I despise you. And if there was a way to ensure my own survival, I would kill you without pause."

That was comforting. I was not sure that I wanted this much honesty from a resident of my head.

"You are a fluke, and one of these days, you are going to do something to get yourself killed. However, I have tried everything I know to either possess you or escape...and I have failed."

What I now heard in Adrianna's voice was something entirely new. It was the ring or defeat. It was clear that I had a steep learning curve ahead, because I had no idea how she had reached these conclusions.

"Our presence here imbues you with the powers that we possess. But there are some things that you need to be aware of before you simply start consuming Supernaturals to gain their power," Blodwen said after a nod from Adrianna. "We must help you master certain functions. For instance, you could not simply create one of the undead without Adrianna—" There was a loud cough that interrupted Blodwen and we all looked to see Cody standing in his doorway once more. Blodwen gave a nod of acknowledgment. "Without Adrianna *or* Cody walking you through the ritual. What you do gain instantly is our innate powers."

"Umm..." I hated to be the idiot, but I was not quite understanding.

"Okay, here is an example," Blodwen spoke with a patience that surprised me. "You were able to step into the Heart of the Sidhe. That is a power that faeries such as I possess naturally."

"You were able to detect zombies," Adrianna added.

Now I was getting it; or, at least I think I was starting to get it. "Okay, so how do I know what these innate powers are?"

"We tell you," both women said in melodic unison.

"And if you don't tell me..." I coaxed.

"Remember that odd sensation that you felt back in Mystify's home?" Adrianna asked. My expression answered in the negative, because she continued to explain, "You picked up on a tingle...that was Morgan's arrival. You sensed another Psychic entering your district uninvited."

And then it clicked. I also understood why she referred to the place as Mystify's home. Yes, Claude had assumed control of it physically, but because Mystify still technically existed, the district still belonged to—

"Crap!" I moaned.

I suddenly understood what it was that Morgan and Betty had been referring to before I jumped home and then Mind-walked my way to understanding.

I was the new Psychic of Dallas!

"I think she just figured it out," Blodwen said with a wryness frosting her words.

"I can't be a Psychic!" I finally said with a pathetic squeak. "I barely know how to be a ghoul."

"We can deal with that later...but that is why we needed Morgan," Adrianna said with more compassion than I have ever heard come from her lips.

"There are ways to handle this," Blodwen added. "But they will be tricky at best, and you will need Morgan to go to the council on your behalf to appeal your appointment. On the down side..." Blodwen gave me a grim look that made me a bit nervous, "...that would officially make Claude the Psychic for that region."

Wow, I thought she was going to say something much worse, like I was going to have to fight somebody to the death or something. Since Claude was basically doing the job already, I did not see the problem. However, the look on that pretty face told me that, as usual, I was missing something in the big picture.

"Okay...spill it. I can tell there is something about this that sucks, and apparently I am not picking up on it," I sighed with what was almost an over-dramatic teenager sound.

I think I had reached my limit on confusion. The past few days had done a lot to make me feel like a total idiot. If you have been following along, you have undoubtedly picked up on that. What I wouldn't give to be in some story where everything made sense and fell into place. Can I just put it out there?

Real life sucks.

"Claude will assume control over everything in his region." Blodwen shot me a raised eyebrow.

Nope...that wasn't helping. I gave the rolling gesture with my hands to indicate that she needed to continue...perhaps give me the "Dick and Jane" version.

*See Ava.*

*See the monsters!*

*See the monsters chase Ava.*

*Run, Ava, Run!*

"Everything in that district will fall under his control. He will have the latitude to make changes as he sees fit."

I puzzled over Blodwen's words for a few seconds, and then an idea began to sprout from the tiny seed. I think my brain needs more water; heaven knows it is full of plenty of fertilizer.

"Theodore?" It was really more of a question.

"He will be under Claude's rule." Blodwen gave a satisfied nod like that teacher who was there at your desk when you finally got those blasted six-times-tables correct for the very first time...including six-times-seven.

"So I just pop back over, pick him up, and anybody else that wants to come, and then I leave." That seemed pretty simple. Right?

"If you return now, you will be bound to that region and have no choice but to assume the role," Blodwen said.

"And Claude will take the role as your lieutenant as he was for Mystify," Adrianna added.

"I don't get a say in this?" As the words came out of my mouth, I realized something else. "And why am I stuck with a lieutenant? Morgan doesn't have one...does she?"

"She did, but her lieutenant died three years ago and she has not replaced him yet," Blodwen said.

"Umm...a few things come to mind here." I pressed my palms to my head, but it was really more out of frustration. I didn't have a headache or anything; it just seemed like the right thing to do. "*He*? Morgan had a male lieutenant? And how in the hell do you know this stuff? Weren't you over in Ireland or something?"

"This is a small community, Ava," Blodwen explained. "It is very easy to keep tabs, and a regional Psychic is a very public figure. Also, you do meet a lot of people over the centuries."

Okay, I could accept that. Still, she had not explained the male lieutenant thing. I gave her the "keep talking" look and crossed my arms over my stomach in a gesture that screamed "I can wait all day!"

"Her lieutenant disappeared just over three years ago." Blodwen finally took the clue.

"You said he died." Yeah, there is a big difference between the two. I wanted the complete answer.

"And that is true. And a few days after his disappearance, his presence simply ceased. Morgan went to the council and there were a few secret meetings that nobody was privy to, so the details are slim. The council made the official declaration the day after Morgan returned to Portland."

"So...what...they send out a mass email? How do they make this declaration? And are you saying there was never a body recovered?"

I thought about that question the moment that it came from my lips. I had seen creatures turn to diamond dust, gloopy piles of yuck, sapphires, and then there were the ones that I devoured. Not much chance of finding any remains in any of those cases. Also, I didn't recall getting any sort of notice when any of the Supernaturals that I knew of had died.

"It is sent to each area Psychic and then they disseminate it how they see fit," Blodwen explained. "Often they simply project the message. Anybody in their district who is affiliated will receive it. For the various species that are not under the umbrella of a Psychic, their leader most likely has a standing agreement to receive the message. I have subscribed to every Psychic around the globe."

"So, do you still get the messages...while you are in my head?"

"Actually...yes."

"Wait! So you have received messages since you have been here?"

"A couple…yes."

"I don't suppose that you care to share those with me."

Then a funny thing happened. Blodwen looked over at Adrianna, and then back to me.

"Not until you learn more control," she said. "I will make the information available to you once you have gotten better at controlling your mind. If I share such things, they are for you and you alone." Again she looked over at Adrianna.

"Just say what you mean," Adrianna scoffed, waving her hand dismissively.

"I don't think it is wise to let *everybody* know *everything*. Some things might be just for you to be made aware. You do show great promise in your skills, and as soon as you can keep your thoughts isolated from us, I will be more forthcoming."

"Wait…you guys can read all my thoughts?"

"Not all of them," Cody said, an edge of cynical sarcasm lacing his voice. "But enough to get a decent idea of what you think about certain things. Of course, all you need to do is take a good look at us to figure out some of the deets."

I shot a withering glance his direction and could swear that he morphed to an even younger version. Oops. Seconds later, he realized it and once again slammed the door to his room. If he wasn't careful, he would end up being about two years old.

I was getting distracted. I had other fish to fry. Notice how I didn't say Bigger? Yeah, that is because I have no idea which fish is the biggest anymore.

"So I can't go back and snatch up Theodore or any of the others who might want to leave…or need my protection? Claude might kill Theodore…and probably those bugbears that pitched in."

I felt a dark sense of unease and dread start to flood me. I had convinced most of the creatures down in that cellar to follow me. I was pretty sure that Claude would dish out some serious amounts of payback.

"He will not be permitted to kill them without a trial," Blodwen said. I saw something flash in her eyes and knew she was not being entirely honest with me.

"If he ruffles so much as one feather—" I began, but Adrianna interrupted.

"You will do nothing. Claude would be the regional Psychic. He would have the protection of his council, and you are going to be busy enough with the Templars."

"Oh yeah!" I spun to face the woman full on. "And I have *you* to thank for that!"

"I would say that you are most welcome, but I detected the sarcasm in your statement." Adrianna took three very bold and confident steps toward me, but I noticed she stayed out of range from any sort of swiping attack I might make.

"You have basically made me the top priority for the Templars. I think I could have been able to work with Race...and now..." My voice trailed off. I could taste the lie on my tongue. Who was I kidding? All I wanted when it came to Race was a good old-fashioned boinking.

"Think with something besides your crotch!" Cody's voice hollered from behind his still-closed door.

"He's right," Blodwen agreed. "While he might not have come for you initially, the fact remains that he is Templar. He would have to choose sooner or later, and he is the kind of man who takes his oath seriously. Perhaps too much so."

"But he's so yummy." My hands clamped over my mouth. Oops. Apparently I have the same problems with my big mouth that I do with my thoughts.

"And as for me making you a priority target for the Templars, I did no such thing. You already held that distinction. What I did was strengthen your power base and also help you save Morgan." Adrianna resumed her defense—such as it was. "Had you stayed in that house, you would have become the Psychic. That would make it impossible for you to run very far if the need should arise...much less hide."

"Hide? Run? Who said anything about running or hiding? But why couldn't I do either of those?"

"You can only stay outside of your district for a period of forty-eight hours." Adrianna tilted her chin, and I turned to Blodwen who was nodding her agreement. "Believe it or not, I was trying to ensure my own preservation. The gwyll was the best chance we had of not only getting out of there, but of saving Morgan."

"Okay…I can totally believe that you were acting in your own selfish interest. No problem there…but I still don't get the whole thing about you wanting to save Morgan."

"And do you think that I could trust you to get yourself out of becoming the Psychic for Dallas?" Adrianna laughed, but not in a good way. It was almost in an evil villainess sort of manner, and it made me actually take a step back. Just that quick, she seemed to assume some form of control over the situation. "You are a bumbling idiot of a child who has only managed to succeed through happenstance. You are easy to distract and possess a gullibility that makes you easy prey for those who wish to bend you to their will."

I wanted to argue…to protest. But hadn't she simply voiced thoughts that I'd held for almost my entire life as a ghoul? I was everything she said…and perhaps worse.

"You would get yourself killed and me in the process," Adrianna spat with a growing vehemence that made me shrink back just a bit more. "I have lived for centuries, and now my future existence is predicated on whether or not you make an easy target of yourself. I will not see my existence come to an end because of you, stupid ghoul."

I felt her words sinking into me and glanced over at Blodwen, expecting to see just more confirmation in her expression that I was a failure. Instead, I saw…sadness? The woman was slumped over and looked as if she could be brought to tears with a single word of disapproval.

A realization struck me with something close to a physical blow and my head popped up to regard Adrianna. She was still glaring at me and had actually seemed to grow a few inches taller. With a sniff and a deep swallow to try and clear my throat so that my voice would not squeak or crack, I took a step closer.

"Then it must really piss you off that I bested you…that I beat you that night in the graveyard." She physically shrank back to her original height. "And then I ate you like so many Cheesy

Poofs!" Now she was a few inches shorter and that beautiful face with its smooth skin was starting to match the hideous and mottled look of her hands. "You live here in my head where I can lock you away any time that I want to. That must really be a blow to an ego like yours."

As I spoke, not only did she shrink down to about half her normal size, but she retreated to her doorway. Let me clarify that. Saying that she retreated might give you the idea that she went of her own free will. Actually, she was sort of dragged back by some unseen force. At last, she was in her room or whatever it was that she occupied in my mind.

"I did what needed to be done for all of us!" Adrianna insisted. I thought I detected a bit of fear in her voice. "The only way you would have been able to help Morgan was to get her in the Heart of a Sidhe."

"And now the Templars will be coming for me with guns blazing."

"That was going to happen no matter what," Adrianna insisted. "And if you think that a few goblins, bugbear, a Psychic and a faerie are all that you need in your power arsenal...you are the fool I assumed you to be!"

"I am not just going to start murdering Supernaturals to gain their powers!" I shouted. "There has to be another way to deal with this."

"Keep saying that...all the way up to the point when a Templar severs your head with a Cold Steel blade and sticks it in a jar for all to see."

I glanced over at Mystify's door. It was like staring at those puzzles that supposedly have hidden three dimensional images that pop out if you stare at them long enough. To quote Joan Rivers, "Can we talk here?" You stare at anything long enough and it will turn into whatever you want. I never did get those stupid things. However, something unraveled for me as I looked at that black goop that appeared to bubble and boil against any laws of physics or logic. Granted, neither of those are my strong suit, but I think you understand what I am saying.

I turned back to the mini-Adrianna and a smile twitched at

the corners of my mouth. I could feel it and did my best to keep it in check. The way her eyes got wide in a hurry let me know that I had been less than successful. Oh well…

Using little more than a force of my will, I slammed Adrianna's door in her face and a sheet of that dark goop poured down the front of the surface. It was not the black like what covered Mystify's door; more like a deep purple that could almost pass for black.

"You are truly a marvel," Blodwen said, awe slipping in to her voice that sounded uncharacteristic in a way.

I turned to face the gwyll. She was still in her Venus form. If anything, she might even be a bit prettier. She had a translucence to her that made her seem to glow a frosty blue and her hair had turned to a snow white; not in the "old lady" way, but something that seemed natural on her and added to her beauty.

"I think I am done here for now." I started to concentrate on spiraling up and out of the rabbit hole.

"Do you think you might make this place a bit more…hospitable before you leave?" Blodwen asked.

I stopped my exit and it almost felt like I fell through a plate glass window. In other words, it was very unpleasant. Somehow I had ended up on the hard stone floor of the large chamber. Getting up, I gave myself a quick inspection and was surprised to discover no cuts, breaks, or even bruises.

"What?" I growled, not in the least bit happy. Deep down, I knew that I couldn't blame Blodwen, this was probably just another skill that I would need to hone.

"Umm…" she took a step back in response to my obvious annoyance. "I apologize…I was just hoping that you could perhaps make this a more comfortable place. As you can see…" she waved her arms around the vast chamber to indicate its barren stone appearance, "…there is little in the ways of comfort. And for somebody like you, I am surprised to see it so bland."

Was she talking about my mind? Was this some sort of representation of how I felt about and saw myself?

"I will make you a deal," I said after giving it some thought.

"Ohhh-kaaay," Blodwen breathed with obvious caution.

"When we met…you told me your name, but said that friends called you Muffy. You don't strike me as a Muffy. So what's the deal?"

Blodwen actually seemed to blush, and then she smiled in perhaps one of the truest smiles that I'd ever seen on her face. Now I was *really* curious.

"When I was young…back before Ireland was called by that name and was known as Hibernia, there was a boy in a village at the base of the hills that I called home. He was a bit of a troublemaker and ran away one day. He entered my pass just as the moon reached its peak and I confronted him, demanding my tribute. He had nothing to give, but I felt sorry for him and promised to spare him if he would perform a few tasks for me. He agreed, and for some inexplicable reason, we actually became friends.

"He was the first human that had not been enthralled by this incarnation that you call my Venus form. He was just a lonely lad and needed a friend. When he completed his tasks, he asked to stay and I allowed it. That was when I revealed my true name to him. It was practice back in those days not to give your real name to mortals for fear that they might be able to use it in a summoning. It turns out that such things only work on demons and leprechauns…"

I wanted to ask a hundred more questions after that last statement, but thought it would be rude to interrupt. I could always ask later.

"…I still remember the frown on his face. He insisted that my name was just not fitting. Like the fool girl that I was, I asked him what would be fitting. He said that I looked more like a 'Murphy' to him.

"As he aged and his teeth fell out, it sounded more like 'Muffy' than anything else. And so that is what I eventually began to use as my name when dealing with humans. Now…if you don't mind?"

I looked around and visualized something a bit more…me.

"Well…I guess that will have to do for now," Blodwen said with just a hint of snobbish disapproval leaking into her tone.

I had no idea what her problem could be with her new digs. Heck, I might come here to visit more often. There were huge neon cityscape pictures on the walls with LED lights that changed color so that it actually looked like the sun rose and set. There was a life-sized poster of the '"Look What the Cat Dragged In" version of Brett on one wall that was lined with an assortment of pinball machines.

Another wall had an array of guitars that were in dazzling shades of pinks, neon greens, purples, and even one that was a beautiful lavender cheetah print. There were video monitors with classic MTV videos playing and an enormous sofa that looked super comfy.

"You should probably get back," Blodwen said.

"I'll keep you out and free to do what you like as long as you don't give me any trouble," I admonished as I sent my thoughts spiraling out. In a bit of reverse vertigo, I was back. I knew it because I was staring up into Aoife's face.

"Get back from her now!" I heard Morgan bark.

Then the pain hit.

Next, on a Very Special *That Ghoul Ava...*

# 17

# I Can't Go For That (No Can Do)

A wave of hunger hit me with a force that I think made me scream. *Somebody* was screaming, of that I was certain.

*Go to my happy place, go to my happy place…*

"You said she was going to be okay," I heard Lisa yell.

"She will be," Morgan said with her matter-of-fact, void-of-any-emotion voice that I was so used to hearing. Glad some things were back to normal.

"She must feed right now."

It took me a moment to run through the voices and connect it with a name. Nose Wart? Memories of the little goblin came back in a rush.

"I have a puppy," I whispered as I sunk into memories of my first dog ever. His name was Pete, and he was a Cocker Spaniel that pretty much hated everybody except me. I still don't believe that my mom "accidentally" left the front door open that day.

The next thing I remember is opening my eyes and seeing the ugliest puppy in the world staring down at me with its red, rheumy eyes, and breath that would melt asbestos.

"Nose Wart," I managed as I tried to sit up. The jangle of metal let me know that I had been chained down.

"Greetings, Just Ava," he answered in his odd voice.

"Where is everybody?" I asked as I looked around and got my bearings.

I felt a pang of longing as the sense of missing my old soundproof basement seeped into my emotional crevices. We'd had to buy this new house out in the freaking boondocks because of—

"Glad you are well," a voice that sounded like boulders being turned to gravel rumbled from my left.

My head jerked over to see a fiery jötunn sitting on the floor beside the bed or table or whatever I was fastened to for some reason that I imagine had more to do with the safety of others than of myself. I still could not tell if it was a boy or a girl, they all had beards that would make ZZ Top go, "Damn!"

"I don't know if I would say that I'm well," I grumbled, flopping back down. "Nose Wart?"

"Yes, Just Ava?"

"Go get somebody to come down here and let me loose from these chains."

I heard what sounded like an agreement and then the flapping of his large, flat feet as he scampered away. I looked up at the ceiling and tried to relax for a moment.

*Glad to have you back*, Blodwen's voice said.

*How long was I out?* I asked.

*No idea.*

I huffed and blew an imaginary strand of hair from my face. There was the sound of a door opening and then somebody running down the stairs.

"Ava!" Lisa squealed and threw herself on me in a hug. I reflexively went to hug her back, only to have my hands come up short. "Let me get those things off you," Lisa said through sobs.

"Thank you." That is what I would have said if a voice did not cut me off before I had the chance.

"What were you thinking?"

"Nice to see you too, Morgan. Oh...wait...I can't see you because I am tied down in some sort of twisted fetish gear." I shook my chains for added effect.

"You were consumed by the *Fame Rabia*," Morgan said as

she appeared above me, her face a pond of Botox placidity. "What made you think it was okay to Mindwalk like that? Or for so long?"

"So long?" I asked. Geez, at the most it had been an hour.

"You were out of it for almost three weeks," Lisa whispered, although I don't know why, Morgan was right beside her and could have probably heard her if she were a block away.

*Three weeks? Wowzers!*

"This only complicates things even more," Morgan announced, cutting off any conversation that Lisa and I might have started.

"How?" Lisa and I asked in unison.

"Who knows that you can do this?" Morgan answered our question with one of her own.

"Nobody?" I answered.

At least I didn't think anybody else knew. Heck, I was trying to keep the fact that I had people living in my head a secret; I sure didn't think that I'd spilled the beans on Mindwalking. However, I was not letting Morgan off the hook that easy.

"So how does this complicate things?" I pressed.

"Because, if the Templars become aware that you are demonstrating all of these powers that have only been suppositions up to this point, they will intensify their quest to kill you," a man's voice said. Race Mitchell stepped into view and I felt my stomach flutter.

"What the hell is he doing here?" I finally managed to blurt. I sure hope that it didn't sound as weak and girly to everybody else as it did in my ears. And what was wrong with me?

Okay…he is super-hot in an outdoorsman, X-Gamer sort of way with his deep tan, strong, square jawline, perfect hair that would make Brad Pitt weep with envy, and eyes so blue that you wanted to drown in them, all wrapped up with lips that were always curved up in the most knowing smile like he had just heard the cleverest joke and knew that you didn't really get it, so he didn't want to laugh and embarrass you.

"Actually," Race said, putting his hands out to stop Lisa who obviously was trying to get him to shut his big, fat mouth,

"I came here to capture you and return you to the Templar High Council."

I heard a low growl joined by a hiss and a deep rumble. Nose Wart, the fiery jötunn, and a bugbear were all suddenly at my side all at once. Each of them had expressions that made it clear what they thought of that possibility.

"But I have decided to hold off," Race added with absolutely no haste or even the slightest hint that he'd heard the menace or threat in the guttural noises of the trio of agitated beasties. "There is something about you that does not add up. I am not convinced that you are some evil spawn of darkness bent on destroying the world."

*No…but I could introduce you to somebody who fit that bill perfectly*, I thought.

Did he have any idea how yummy he looked? And not in a way that involved Sharkmouth. I was talking about that polo shirt that stretched across a broad chest that I just knew a ghoul could sink her head into and nuzzle. And his arms filled every centimeter of the sleeve to the point where you could see that the material was straining just a bit around those bulging biceps. Hmm…wonder if I am suffering from *Fame Hornia*?

Lisa frowned and I knew that I'd missed something. Oh…and Morgan was gone. I know that most adventures end with all the questions answered…but not this one. This one ends with me standing at the crossroads with more questions than when it started. So much has changed in such a short time. Something told me that I was now an official member of the Supernatural community.

I am a killer.

I am a monster.

I am That Ghoul Ava.

**MAY DECEMBER**
Publications

**The growing voice in horror
and speculative fiction.**

Find us at www.maydecemberpublications.com
Or
Email us at contact@maydecemberpublications.com

His blog can be found at:http://twbrown.blogspot.com

The best way to find everything he has out is to start at his Amazon Author Page:http://www.amazon.com/TW-Brown/e/B00363NQI6

You can follow him on twitter @maydecpub and on Facebook under Todd Brown, Author TW Brown, and also under May December Publications.

TW Brown is the author of the *Zomblog* series, his horror comedy romp, ***That Ghoul Ava***, and, of course...the ***DEAD*** series. Safely tucked away in the beautiful Pacific Northwest, he moves away from his desk only at the urging of his Border Collie, Aoife. (Pronounced Eye-fa)

He plays a little guitar on the side...just for fun...and makes up any excuse to either go trail hiking or strolling along his favorite place...Cannon Beach. He answers all his emails sent to twbrown.maydecpub @gmail.com and tries to thank everybody personally when they take the time to leave a review of one of his works.

www.ingramcontent.com/pod-product-compliance
Lightning Source LLC
Chambersburg PA
CBHW070325130626
46556CB00007B/2730